The American Hobbit

The American Hobbit

G. Ellis Wheeler

Writers Club Press
San Jose New York Lincoln Shanghai

The American Hobbit

All Rights Reserved © 2001 by George Ellis Wheeler

No part of this book may be reproduced or transmitted in any form or by any means, graphic, electronic, or mechanical, including photocopying, recording, taping, or by any information storage retrieval system, without the permission in writing from the publisher.

Writers Club Press
an imprint of iUniverse.com, Inc.

For information address:
iUniverse.com, Inc.
5220 S 16th, Ste. 200
Lincoln, NE 68512
www.iuniverse.com

ISBN: 0-595-16828-0

Printed in the United States of America

*To Emily
with affection,
George*

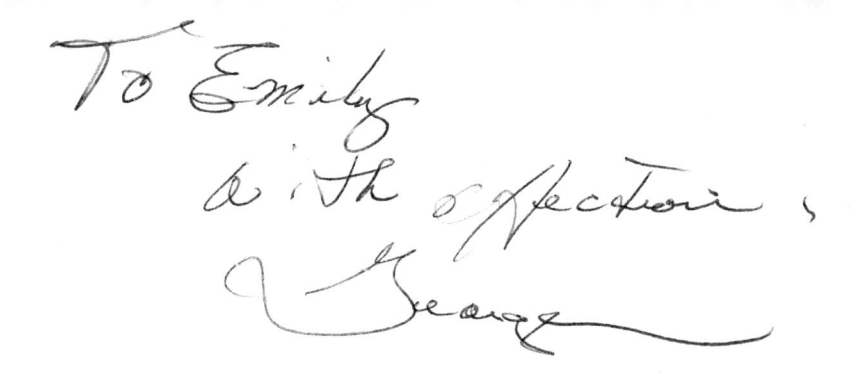

Dedicated to elaine and jean, two great librarians who turned copy editor, agent and critic out of heart.

The train's six engines pulled slowly around the high mountain curves. Bare cliffs, carved by the whispers of time, shut out the eastside view from the boxcar. The west side was scenic, but scary, because of the five-hundred foot drop-off.

"Heck of a ways down," noted California Red to anyone listening. He stood at the boxcar door, looking out, mostly, but sometimes down.

"Them darn Mormons know how to mess up a railroad, I'd say," chipped in Jack Frost.

"Wasn't the Mormons," Hobbit corrected. "They hired Chinese, and they're the ones messed the thing up."

Mary the woman sat in the back of the boxcar. She watched the three men, listening as they argued the merits and demerits of railroads and who was responsible for them. She wished the train would go faster so it would get to Salt Lake before dark, but she knew it wouldn't. She had been on the road for over three years. She knew what the men on the road wanted when darkness fell. Maybe one of them would have some wine. Hobbit, maybe. He looked like the sort that could save some wine. She wouldn't try to fight. Not even argue. She'd quit that a long time ago.

At the top of Soldiers' Summit the engines stopped. The helper engines unhooked and the main engines started up again. The train of boxcars, loaded with merchandise from the east, began its downward descent toward Salt Lake City.

Darkness invaded the empty boxcar carrying the four travelers. Talk among the three men lessened, then stopped. Hobbit reached under his heavy trench coat, a glimmer of moonlight revealing his hand withdrawing a fifth of Thunderbird. The woman Mary was glad there were only three of them. Commonly, there were ten men for every woman on the road.

The wine was good, and, because it was Hobbit's and he said so, Mary the woman drank two drinks to the men's one until it was gone.

Hobbit was different. Men up and down the road respected him. Some, from the sixties and seventies, feared him.

Soon, another bottle of Thunderbird appeared from under Hobbit's coat, and it wasn't long until the three men and Mary the woman were too drunk to do anything but go to sleep. The train stopped briefly at Provo to drop off some boxcars, then headed on to Salt Lake City. When it stopped in the freight yard at Salt Lake, the four groggily awake passengers got off.

Mary the woman picked Hobbit to follow. California Red and Jack Frost headed for Pioneer Park. "I'll carry some of your stuff," Mary the woman offered. "Nah," Hobbit replied. "I have to stay used to what I can carry. That way I always know where I am with it."

"You're smarter than most men of the road," Mary the woman told him. "Not smarter," Hobbit replied. "Just pay more attention to what I am doing."

"You going to get some more wine?" she asked him. "I've got more wine," he told her. "For later. First we find a place to take a bath."

She didn't say anymore. She had heard about Hobbit, how he was different from other men on the road and would do what he set his mind to do before he did anything else. Most people on the road didn't stay with Hobbit long because of that. Most people on the road wanted to get drunk, eat and fornicate, and they didn't always arrange them in any sort of order. Getting drunk, though, could take priority over the other two.

It was a long walk all the way uptown from the freight yard. Soon, they were next to the City Hall. There was a motel across the street. Hobbit stopped. He looked at the motel for at least a full minute.

"No good," he said. But he crossed the street there and kept on walking.

Three blocks south, many motels and hotels began to appear. Hobbit kept on walking. He turned at one corner, then another. He seemed to be going around in an odd circle. Then he stopped and put down his road gear.

Mary the woman had only a bedroll made of a quilt and blankets. She had one change of clothes in it. Except socks. She only had the one pair of socks she had on. She had gotten the change of clean clothes from a Rescue Mission and they didn't have any socks. They hardly ever had socks at Rescue Missions.

"Put my stuff behind those bushes," Hobbit told her, then added, "Yours, too."

The bushes were shrubs, planted at the rear of the motel to block off the dullness of its flat, windowless back wall.

Hobbit watched her put the gear away. Satisfied she had done a good job, he stepped closer to her and asked, "You ever done this before?" She shook her head negatively.

"You wait down here till I find a room," he told her, "Then I'll come back and get you."

He walked briskly toward a high rise balconied motel. Spotting an ornamental flower pot under a second floor balcony, he sprinted toward it, and, with an agility that belied his forty years, leaped up on the pot and grabbed the floor of the balcony. One swing and he kipped up on the porch. Bad luck. He could see that the room was occupied because the curtains were pulled. No light. They were asleep.

He quickly crossed the balcony and stood at the edge. He would have to jump several feet to the next balcony. He jumped. Still no luck. When he crossed the balcony this time, he could see the glare of a television coming from the room. "Darn!" he thought to himself. "Darn!"

He stood hard against the building and stepped up on the balcony rail, then he reached up and put both hands flat on the third floor balcony. Slowly, he pulled himself up.

Luck! The curtains weren't drawn, and there was no light.

Agilely he jimmied the sliding glass panel door open and stepped into the room. He quickly checked the closets for luggage. There was none. To make doubly sure, he checked the bathroom to see if a towel or wash rag had been used. None had.

He went back to the balcony, going down the left side to avoid the room where the t-v was on. He was sure he could push Mary the woman up the two balconies. She was sober again.

He looked around carefully before dropping off the second floor balcony. No one was in sight. Briskly, he walked to where he had left Mary the woman and his road gear. Mary the woman was not there. When he checked behind the bushes, he could see that his bag had been opened. The bottle of wine was gone.

Hobbit fished through the pack and found a clean change of clothes. Rolling them up, he tied them in a shirt, then around his neck. In a few minutes, he was back in the motel room taking a hot shower.

He wouldn't risk turning the t-v on, not even with the sound off. Security persons might open the door for any number of reasons, and it was possible they might check into the room. When he had rolled his dirty clothes up tightly, he took a bag out of one of the small trash containers in the room and put the clothes into it. Then he searched through the items he had taken out of his pockets and laid them on the bedside table.

Finding his watch with no wristband, he checked the time. Two a.m. Not bad so far. He would stay awake. A call to the kitchen around 5 a.m. would be about right. The desk person would not notice which room it came from.

After putting the watch in his shirt pocket, then the remaining items in his pants pockets, he stepped into the bathroom and turned the light off, relying entirely now on the glitter of early morning in the big city.

Finding the least-lighted spot on the balcony side of the bed, he lay down and relaxed.

It felt good to be clean. It was good to have clean clothes and underwear and socks. He could almost go to sleep, but he wouldn't. He had done this many times before.

After a while, he reached into his shirt pocket and withdrew the watch. Eight minutes to five. He got up.

Fumbling, he found the nightstand with the telephone on it. Beside the phone was the phone book. He took it to the bathroom.

Turning on the bathroom light with one hand, he closed the door with the other. Luck! The house phone directory was on the phone book cover. 236–Kitchen. 236, he repeated the numbers over to himself. He turned the bathroom light off. Fumbling again, he made his way back to the telephone. The dial light came on when he picked up the receiver. He dialed 236.

"Kitchen," a voice answered.

"What time will you start serving breakfast," he asked.

"At five-thirty," the voice said.

"Thank you," he told the voice, and cradled the phone.

He went back to the bathroom. This time he closed the door before turning on the light. From his pocket he withdrew a small birthday candle, a metal gallon jar top and a small bottle. The bottle contained gasoline.

He had to search to find his miniature cigarette lighter, but, after finding it, he proceeded with making his incendiary device.

First, he melted some of the candle into the metal jar lid. Then he stood the candle up in its own wax. After making sure the candle was firmly anchored, he poured in the gasoline. Then he took the wash rag he had used and began wiping everything he had touched. He had relaxed too much in bathrooms to rely on his sliding touch method of distorting his fingerprints.

He looked at his watch. Twelve minutes after five. He decided to have a bowel movement. Something to kill time. He had a good one before taking his shower. The wine had done that. But he could always use another one, if anything was there. Nothing was there. He wiped, anyway, then decided to take the roll of paper off the roller. He would put it with the phone book.

He grabbed a towel and used it to open the bathroom door. Picking up the phone book, toilet paper and metal gallon jar top, he took them to the bed. There he placed all of them under the bed. Then he gathered up the trash bag with the dirty clothes in it. When he went back to the bathroom to turn the light out, he quickly surveyed everything in the room and recalled his actions. He was satisfied he had left no real evidence that could be traced to him. Then he reached into his pocket and produced the miniature cigarette lighter. He lit the candle. After making sure it was well lit, he went to the door, opened it, and went to the elevator.

Downstairs, he looked first for the lounge door. Sometimes the cleanup people left it unlocked. He found it and checked the door. Luck! It was unlocked!

Inside the lounge, the lights were out. He deposited his trash bag full of dirty clothes and other items in the lounge, then proceeded to the dining room and ordered breakfast.

Hobbit had eaten his pancake and was cutting his fork into one of the over-easy eggs when he heard the wail and honk of fire engines. Soon the hotel was in bedlam. Employees were running around everywhere. Guests were streaming out into the street. Four different people had told him the place was on fire.

He finished his breakfast. After wiping his mouth and hands well with the cloth napkin, he headed toward the lounge door. Inside, it was still dark. He fumbled for his lighter. Finding it, he withdrew it and lit it for just a second in order to get his bearings. Then he picked up his bag of dirty clothes and other items and headed for the overhead t-v on the back outer wall. Finding the set, he felt blind-man style for the "on" button. When the t-v came on, he set the volume all the way off.

As he moved to the bar, he could see everything he needed to see in the light of the t-v. At a dirty towel disposal he dropped off his own dirty towel. Then he began filling the vacated area of the bag with whiskey. The cigarette machine had been unplugged, and he had a problem locating it, but, finding it in a far corner, he went to it and jimmied open the lock with the "Made in Pakistan" Bowie knife he carried in a scabbard inside his pants. There was some money in the coin box. He took that, along with an uncounted number of packs of cigarettes.

His sack was full and getting just a little bit heavy. Another trash bag would make things better. He looked but couldn't find one. Darn! He couldn't risk walking out with the thing and have it bust open. There was a mob of people out there. They might kill him.

Quickly, he dumped everything out of the trash bag onto the floor. Then he tied up one leg of his dirty pants. Into the leg he stuffed the liquor and cigarettes, putting everything else back into the bag.

Holding tightly to the bag and pants leg, he walked toward the outside fire exit door. As he passed the t-v, he cut it off.

Hobbit cracked open the fire exit door slightly in order to listen to the sounds outside. The voices told him that the firemen had put the room fire out. Now he would have to move very fast before a fire marshal went to work determining the cause of the blaze.

Pushing the door open further, he sighed and relaxed momentarily as the first breath of cool early-morning air filled his lungs. Then, with a burst of enthusiastic determination, he pushed open the door, and walked briskly across and down the street to the bushes that sheltered his tent and pack.

He transferred the liquor and cigarettes to his pack, took the knot out of the dirty pants and threw them, along with the shirt, under the bushes. He could buy better clean ones from a thrift store for as much as it would cost him to launder them.

When he had everything together he headed toward Pioneer Park.

Hobbit sat down under the bridge out in the west end of the park. His mind mulled over the bodies lying around, some under blankets, sleeping bags, old coats. There has to be a better way, he thought to himself. Somehow there has to be a way out. He had tried a Rescue Mission once. He took the ear beating, went for the nose-dive, and got in on the staff. They made him the laundry man. Bible lesson every day. It seemed that the people who ran the place believed in God, but they didn't seem to understand Him. They thought they had God figured out. He shook his head at the thought. "Who could figure out a real God", he almost said aloud.

An old car pulled up on the north side of the park and stopped. Two young black men and a black girl got out. They were small time drug dealers. People in the park were beginning to wake up. A few had money to buy an early morning upper drug. The drugs were pills, stolen, mostly, and they sold for a dollar to three dollars each. The three pushers would pick up a couple of hundred dollars altogether.

Hobbit had figured out how he could rob the three drug dealers, but he declined because he felt there was too much risk for a little bit of money. He had seen on t-v a real drug raid on a kingpin's house. The narcs had found a million dollars in cash hidden in an artificial tree in the living room. That would be worth the risk, he thought seriously. That would be worth the risk.

"Hey, Hobbit," the voice of California Red broke into his thoughts. He turned around.

"You got a drink on you, man?" Red asked wantingly.

"Sure," Hobbit replied. "And I need to talk to you about something."

"You got something up?" asked California Red as he took the mini bottle proffered him.

"Sort of," Hobbit replied. "And I need you to find Jack Frost and Mary the woman," he told Red. "I'll need all of you."

"Why her?" demanded California Red. "She ripped you off last night. She told us she did. She was drunk as a skunk."

"I like girls and women," Hobbit told him. "For me they can do no wrong."

"You might better think about it," California Red warned. "Specially if you're thinking about doing something heavy. I'm not trying to make you mad—no way I'd do that. But you might have a little something wrong with your thinking on that."

"I like all girls and women," Hobbit spoke sternly. "And to Hades with any right that makes it wrong." By noon California Red was back with

Jack Frost and Mary the woman. The four of them sat down on the ground forming a kind of circle. Hobbit reached into his pack and withdrew three mini bottles of whiskey which he laid in the middle of the circle. Putting his hand back into the pack he produced a package of cigarettes, laying them on the ground also.

When all had finished their whiskey, Hobbit spoke.

"We can all make a lot of money," he told them, "if we are willing to risk our lives for it."

"Heck," spoke up Jack Frost, "I was born to die."

"I want to live to spend all that money," retorted California Red.

"I'll try anything to get out of this mess I'm in," said Mary the woman flatly.

"We're going to need two more women," Hobbit told them.

"What are we going to do, Hobbie?" asked Jack Frost.

"Can't tell you," Hobbit replied, then added "and don't call me Hobbie again. I'm no sissy."

"Hobbit," spoke up California Red. "You're not planning to steal something from the proving grounds, are you?"

"No," he said. "We're going to Florida. And we'll need two more women. Now get out there and find two more women—something like Mary the woman."

Hobbit knew of a place where he could stash his things. It was an old abandoned boxcar near the freight yard, so he headed out that way. It would be morning before they settled on two women, and he knew of a good buffet style restaurant he wanted to check out.

Dusk was falling gently over Salt Lake City as Hobbit made his way from the freight yard toward the restaurant. Arriving there, he headed around back to where the service door would be. Just off the property there was a hedgerow and a utility shed abutting the hedge. Here Hobbit set up for waiting. You could always bank on these Mormons, he thought to himself. They don't like smoking inside their businesses. So he would watch till a smoker would come out the back door and he would get a peek inside.

Sure enough, a young woman came outside, putting something on the floor to block the door from locking her out.

Hobbit had watched closely. It looked pretty good so far.

Between then and nine-thirty, several people came out to smoke, and Hobbit had gotten a very good mental picture of the kitchen. At nine-thirty he walked around to the front door. Entering, he walked straight to the kitchen. The restaurant closed at ten. By eleven all employees would be gone. Although it was a large restaurant, this kind never used inside security at night. Hiding, he began his hour-and-a-half wait.

When the lights finally went out in the kitchen, Hobbit began pushing his way out from under the pile of day-old bread. He knew about the bread. They gave it to the Rescue Mission. Every other day a driver in the Mission who had a valid driver's license would come down and pick it up. What was still usable was fed to the poor and homeless who came to the Mission to eat. The rest was given to a man who raised hogs. He gave the Mission a hog each year at Christmas.

Making his way in the dark to one of the two swinging doors, Hobbit stood and watched for a while. Soon, he saw the last light from the office go out and heard the click of the door locking.

He gave the manager time to drive off, then proceeded to the dining room. After surveying the perimeter, he made sure no cars remained in the parking lot. He then checked the office for light coming under the door. None was. After checking the two restrooms, he headed back to the kitchen.

The kitchen was pitch dark and he had to grope his way around. Finally, his hand felt the door handle of the walk-in cooler. He snapped the door open slightly, but not all the way. Readying himself into position, he quickly opened the door just enough to get in and plunged abruptly inside the lighted cooler, snatching the door closed behind him.

Hobbit was hungry. He began feeling of pans, checking them for warmth. Pulling a loaf of day old bread from under his coat, he began making sandwiches from the still-warm leftovers of meat. When he had made six large ones, he took a gallon of milk and made his way into the dining room where streetlights provided just enough to see by. There he fell in behind a table and began to eat.

When he finished the milk and sandwiches he was full and, as he relaxed, he felt just a little tired. But after a few minutes he pulled himself together and headed toward the office. Checking the door, he found it locked, so he turned back to the kitchen to get burglar tools.

Returning with knives, sharpeners, and large meat hammers, he began breaking through the office door. As soon as he entered the office he closed the door and turned the light on. The first thing he spied was a medium-size office safe. Luck! He returned to the kitchen. Risking the lights on, he dashed around getting meat cleavers and anything else that was large and heavy enough to cut through the safe door. Loaded down, he managed to turn the kitchen lights off before returning to the office. To be on the careful side he surveyed the perimeter outside from the dining room. Finding nothing suspicious, he returned to the office. He selected the heaviest meat cleaver—about five pounds—and, after turning the safe to give him a better swinging point, he began chopping a slit into the safe's door. The work was arduous and loud, prompting him to stop every once in a while and go out into the dining room to survey the perimeter.

Finally, the heavy blade stuck. He had made a hole! Twisting the meat cleaver back and forth, he managed to widen the cut enough to force the edge of the cleaver's blade into it. With the heavy meat hammer he began driving the meat cleaver downward toward the tumblers. After awhile he was there. Jerking the cleaver out, he inserted a large chef's knife and began poking it into the fireproofing that surrounds the tumblers. When he heard the tumblers fall, he turned the handle on the door and the door opened.

The cash register drawer was full of money. Opening money for the next morning. When he picked it up he saw a cloth bank bag which was laden with rolls of pennies, nickels, dimes and quarters. Underneath the cloth bag he found a plastic bank bag with packs of one and five dollar bills. Frantically, he began pulling everything out of the safe. Maybe someone was skimming off the top! Leaving the money in the safe until a later day. No soap. There was no more money in the safe, but he was so elated by his first finds that he could feel no disappointment. He put all of the money in the cloth bag.

His final act in the office was to withdraw a small plastic bag of cigarette butts from his coat pocket and begin lighting them. They were all the same brand and about the same size. As he got them burning good, he snubbed them out on the desktop and the safe. No better way to beat the man than to leave him a clue. What an admixture of DNA that must be! Piling the kitchen tools into the "out" tray on the desk, he picked it up with one hand and the money with the other and headed back to the kitchen. He rarely worried about fingerprints. If you moved your hands right, you would leave only smudges, no prints.

Retracing his steps, he cleaned up any clue that a tramp had been there. The morning crew wouldn't know what leftovers the evening crew had left. At least they wouldn't come down to the tracks looking for the burglar.

The morning was beginning to make its way into the night when Hobbit decided to take the chance and leave. Traffic was beginning to pick up, and if he could make it across the road without a cop seeing him he would have it made. It would be a few minutes after he triggered the burglar alarm before the police arrived, and they would have to wait on a key to get in. By that time, he would be long gone.

When Hobbit arrived at the abandoned freight car the morning sun had already risen over the great Mormon Temple and was shedding its brightness over the Great Salt Lake. He climbed into the freight car, checked his pack and stretched out full length. He was tired. Very tired.

His mind turned nostalgically back many years before, and he wondered how things might have been.

When he awoke he was late for the meeting in the park and he knew it. He had been very tired and that kind of sleep knew no time. He felt refreshed, alive, and well. Going to the boxcar door, he relieved himself outside, but decided he could save number two until he could use a restroom up town. Putting the money in his coat pockets, he headed out for the park.

The weather was cooling off, and the people in the park were huddling together. Pretty soon the snows would begin and the park would be empty. The homeless who had stayed there would find something warmer for the winter. One or two would deliberately get drunk and sock a cop in order to get enough time in jail to allow them to eat and be warm for the winter. Some would try Rescue Missions, but the Missions were strict, and a lot of the people who had tried them and flunked out wouldn't go back. Others would try the Salvation Army, and those who knew about them and got in early would go to one of the Catholic retreats. During the cold, sometimes freezing winters, some would turn to more serious crimes in an attempt to obtain food and shelter. Those who got caught went to the state prison with long prison sentences.

"Hey, Hobbit," Jack Frost had seen him first and called out.

Hobbit waved to them, noticing that they had two additional women.

"Hobbit," said Jack Frost, "This is Little Debbie, and this is Screaming Girl." They're all right, and they want to come in with us." "Ya'll know what you're getting yourselves into?" asked Hobbit. "This is a hard, life-risking thing."

"I understand it," Little Debbie spoke up, and Screaming Girl joined in with "I know you, Hobbit."

"OK," Hobbit told them, "I'll take Mary the woman." He was leaving the found women to those who had found them. Both were three-mixed: Black, White and Indian. They didn't do so well in the straight world unless they were adopted into solid middle class families. Sometimes a pretty one would get by, or one with a high intelligence. But none of this seemed to apply to Screaming Girl or Little Debbie, which was for the best.

Mary the woman stepped over beside Hobbit and looked at him. Neither had a committal look, but both understood. Between the two of them, they by far out-experienced any other pair, and that left them in control.

The other four had stepped away for a bit of privacy. Now they returned. Little Debbie was with California Red and Screaming Girl was with Jack Frost.

"OK. I've got a few mini bottles of whiskey left," Hobbit told them, "So why don't we have one, then go get something to eat."

All agreed it was a good idea, and they sat down on the grass. Again, they formed a sort of circle, and Hobbit set out five bottles this time. He also set out two packs of cigarettes.

"Now," Hobbit had their attention, "Do you know how to shop lift?" When all confirmed that they did, he continued. "Screaming Girl, how do you shop lift?"

"I just stick whatever it is down in my panties and walk out," she told him.

"Have you ever been busted for shop lifting?" he asked her.

"Yes!" she replied.

"Well, how about you, Little Debbie?" he asked her.

"Yes," she told him.

"Well," Hobbit began, "I'm going to tell you, and then I'm going to show you, how to greatly diminish your risk of getting caught."

"Now, first of all," he continued, "You find the plastic baggies; then you open a pack of one gallon baggies, take them out of the box, and hide them somewhere on you. Follow me and watch everything I do. But first, let me warm you about coffee. It's best to get instant coffee, because fresh coffee has a very strong aroma."

The six walked up the street to an Albertson's supermarket. Inside, they went to work. After each had gotten a handful of baggies, Hobbit went to the section where the coffee was kept. He took out a baggie and put it on the shelf below. Taking down a large jar of instant coffee, he screwed off the lid and poured the coffee into his baggie. After replacing the empty jar, he zipped up the baggie and hid it inside his coat. On the top shelf were bottles of creamer, and he put one of them in Little Debbie's baggie. At the sugar shelf, taking a two-pound bag, he got Screaming Girl in the act. Then they headed to the packaged meat section where Hobbit produced a single-edged razor blade. As he cut open the packs of meat, he handed some to everybody, two packs each. With that, he went to the bread aisle and picked up two loaves and added a jar of sandwich spread as he headed to the cashier. When he had paid for the bread and spread, he started for he door, but just as he reached the door, Screaming Girl and Little Debbie passed him and, at that instant, the security alarm went off. Hobbit put his arm around Mary the woman to stop her, and they and the two other men separated from the two women who had set the alarm off.

"We'll all go back to the boxcar," Hobbit told them. "If they don't get caught they'll be there."

Sure enough, they were there, and Hobbit led them to the abandoned boxcar. There they sat on the floor and began putting their food in a common pool. Each of the two new women put a small can of cooked ham in the pile. Hobbit didn't say anything. He just opened the two cans, put the meat in a baggie, walked to the boxcar door, and threw the two cans as far as he could. Then, reaching into his pack, which he had retrieved from the park, he produced his coffee making apparatus. "Red," he spoke, "You and Jack take this plastic jug down to the rail yard and get some water. You know where it is. And take those two ham cans I just threw out and throw them a little further."

While the two men were gone, Hobbit put the three women to making sandwiches. Soon the sandwiches were made, the water hot, and they passed Hobbit's World War II metal Army cup around, sipping the steaming warmer-upper as they stuffed their faces.

When everyone had gotten enough, Hobbit put the women to cleaning up and saving the leftovers. He spoke softly to California Red and Jack Frost, and they left the boxcar, walking slowly.

When they were off a piece, Hobbit spoke, "This sure is a hard thing for me to say, but those two women might not work out. They took those two cans of ham with the electronic markings on them, believing they were doing something good for us. And we sure can't have that. They'll get us killed. Since they're your women, what do you think?"

California Red was the first to speak. "I like mine, and I'd like to keep her. It's a long time between here and Florida and I believe they can learn."

Jack Frost spoke up for Screaming Girl. "Mine ain't too smart, but she cares, and that counts for a lot of smarts. I say we keep them."

"OK," agreed Hobbit. "But if they aren't in line when we get to Florida, then all we've done is gone to Florida. I'm not going to let anyone get me killed. I come close enough myself." In agreement, the three men headed back inside the boxcar. As they stepped in through the door, the women became silent and looked toward them.

Jack Frost spoke up. "Ya'll are all right. We appreciate you thinking enough of us to get that ham, and, the truth is, you didn't get caught. But we need to either pull out of this thing or let one mind run it. Hobbit is a smart man and he has been around. I'm sure he will ask our advice when it is needed. I'm sure, too, that he won't expect us to go into anything without our knowing what we are doing."

Screaming Girl thanked Jack Frost and both of them smiled at each other. Little Debbie smiled at California Red, because she knew he had spoken up for her. Mary the woman felt comfortable with Hobbit and knew her position in the group was secure.

When they had finished eating, all but Hobbit, who didn't smoke, had a cigarette, then set about getting things together to start heading out to find an empty freight car going south. Finished, all of them saluted Salt Lake City, waved good bye, then jumped out of the track side of the boxcar and headed to the rail yard to find themselves an empty freight car. All six of them were experienced at hoboing, and the first thing they did was find a train yardman to ask him about a train headed southeast. When they got the right track and located it, they began pairing off, two heading toward the outer side of the freight yard heading south, two heading toward the outer side of the yard heading north, the other two taking the center.

It was Jack Frost who made the hobo call. It sounded more like the howl of a lonesome wolf on a foggy mountaintop. Three raps with a track pin on a freight car followed the call. All four of the others began running south. The three raps meant that the train was already engined up, ready to pull out.

Six engines! It was a long train. Counting the stop they would make in Provo, it would probably be daylight before they would get to Helper.

They knew Helper would be their first stop, because there was a Rescue Mission there. They would need the blankets and warm clothes they could get for going over the Rocky Mountains. None of the five had bedrolls or warm clothes, but Hobbit had some miniature fire logs that he shared with them; he also let them swap his big coat around and wrap up in his tent. He had a warm bed roll, a heavy-duty sleeping bag, insulated on the outside with a body bag. He had gotten the body bag in San Francisco at a body bag factory. Some of the men talking outside had given it to him.

Although the snows had not begun, it was cold on top of Soldiers' Summit. Over seven thousand feet with a high chill factor, Soldiers' Summit posed a late fall to early spring problem each year. A lot of people wouldn't even think about driving over it if it was snowing, although the snowploughs kept the roads clear.

By morning, the six travelers were pulling into the freight yard at Helper. When the train stopped, they jumped off and headed toward Main Street. Almost immediately a Helper City Policeman driving a squad car drove up and turned his blue light on. All six of them started to run, thinking the thing in Salt Lake had followed them there, but they saw that the policeman was young and in obviously good physical condition, so they waited.

Officer Pat Elam got out of his car, hand on gun holster, and walked toward the group of homeless people. "I'm Officer Pat Elam," he told them. "I want to know how long you people plan to stay in Helper. I also want to advise you that regardless of how long you stay you may not come into the city for any reason. When you get ready to leave, you walk the tracks back to the freight yard and catch your train out. Do all of you understand that?"

"We all do," Mary the woman assured him. "You won't have any trouble out of us."

"I hope not," said Officer Elam, with a warning in his voice. "Now. How long do you plan to stay?"

"We're going to Florida," Hobbit told him. "And we hoped to get some warm clothes and five bedrolls to make it over the Rockies with."

"Can any of you cook?" Officer Elam asked.

"I can," California Red spoke up.

"Well, they need a cook at the Mission right now, so if you will help them out I will let all of you stay for a while. Otherwise, be out of Helper in three days or I'll arrest you on suspicion and put you in the county jail in Price. Now, if you will get back on the tracks and walk north for about three quarters of a mile, you'll see the Christian Rescue Mission and the Carbon County Emergency Homeless Shelter. The director is Harley Laws. You'll like him. He is a good man."

"What ever happened to Rev. Jim who ran the Mission that used to be on Main Street?" asked Jack Frost. "He was a good man and I liked him."

"He and his wife live in a converted Airstream trailer on the north end of the new Mission. He doesn't get around much now, but you will see him. The best thing for you to do is tell Brother Harley you would like to work with the cattle. Rev. Jim and his wife are in charge of that and they are always in need of help."

Everyone thanked Officer Elam and headed back to the tracks, turning north at first sight of the freight yard. They could ease over to the tracks as they walked, but right now they wanted to get to that Mission.

Sure enough, almost a mile up the tracks they spotted the Mission. It was spread out all over the place and they were very impressed. From the point where they came in, they could see the animals—sheep, goats, a few cows and mules, and some yard animals, chickens and geese. Toward the center was a new brick building with wings. Around it children were playing.

"Wonder what they've got down there?" Hobbit exclaimed. "Where did all those kids come from?"

"On the streets in Salt Lake they are taking homeless children and putting them somewhere," Screaming Girl told him. "I heard it's pretty nice. So that could be what that is."

Little Debbie held her peace. She knew that was what that was. It had been in the newspapers. The whole Mission complex had cost over a million dollars, and they had a professional fund raising organization funding it. It was well endowed.

When they entered the Mission property, they turned down to the west of the property to walk by the Price River. The water was very clean and its swift rush exposed it for a trout stream. In many ways, this was a kid's paradise. Spotting a sign that said "Office," they turned up hill and headed toward it.

As they entered the office, they were met by a very sweet woman about sixty years old. "My name is Bertha," she told them. "I run this end of things during the day. Now, if you sign the book and put your social security numbers on it, I will find you a bed."

When she turned the admission ledger toward them, each in turn signed it.

"The cop up town said you need a cook," questioned California Red. "If you do, can all of us stay?"

"Sure," Bertha told him. "And the rest of you can go out to the ranch and help the preacher and his wife. They are desperately in need of some people to do some cleaning up out there."

"How far is the ranch from here?" asked Little Debbie.

If you came from town up the tracks, you saw it," Bertha replied. "Down where those sheep, goats and other things are."

"Hell of a big ranch," cracked Jack Frost.

Bertha looked at him fiercely and scolded, "You don't use profanity around here, not if you plan to stay more than three days. We will give anyone three days just to show them that God loves them. But after three days you have to start acting like a Christian. In the meantime, you can stay down there next to the highway in the Homeless Emergency Shelter. It's funded by the government, so we don't have any say about it. Just manage it. Brother Harley swung the deal, just for people like you, thinking, maybe, you might take a notion to seek the Lord."

She then picked up the red telephone, and, after a second or two, spoke someone's name and cradled the receiver.

"Esther will be up here in a minute," Bertha told them. "You just have yourselves a cup of coffee and a seat."

Getting back to her business of tabulating the roster for yesterday, Bertha paid no attention to Esther when she arrived and introduced herself. But before they could get out the door she called out, "You've got one for the Shelter. The cusser."

As she drove down to the Shelter, Esther introduced them to another rule. "We don't allow any kind of standard vehicle on the property inside of the outside parking lots. That little wagon you are riding in was made especially for hauling people around in. We also have some small tractors with snowploughs on them."

Arriving at the Shelter, Esther pulled up in front of a door marked office. A woman came out and told them that she was the Shelter manager and that they could call her Fishmouth.

Immediately Screaming Girl squealed, "Do you remember me, Fishmouth? I went to Wendover with you and two guys one time."

"Lordy, Samantha," replied Fishmouth. "I sure do."

"They call me Screaming Girl now," she informed Fishmouth.

"Well, that doesn't matter here," the Shelter manager told her. "Here the Lord reigns supreme, and everything takes a back seat to that. If you stay around for a while we will be seeing more of each other."

After Jack Frost had gotten off, Esther turned the ATV around and headed back across the river, going left, then north. In a few minutes she stopped in front of two rock buildings. The buildings had once been much farther towards town, but they had been moved out to the ranch.

"Ok." Esther shouted back to them, "All men off. The house closest to the barn is empty. You will profit if you take it. Both houses have two bathrooms with showers and tubs, but there is only one room left in the one closest to the office."

When she had deposited the two men, she drove the three women to a mobile home with instructions that they would have to decide who got which room. So far, Fishmouth fell into idle thinking, all of the people, including herself, had come from the streets and knew how Missions were operated. That Jack Frost fellow had been around, and he must have made Bertha mad about something.

Around eleven-thirty, Bertha called the rock house and told Hobbit that lunch would be ready in thirty minutes. She called the mobile home with the same message.

At noon, the fare was soup and sandwiches. The cook, a woman, told them that they could have all the soup and sandwiches they wanted. She also spoke to California Red, telling him she would need him about three o'clock that afternoon to help with the evening meal.

After three days, Jack Frost was let out of the emergency shelter. Later, he was moved into the rock house with the other two men.

Being residents, they all had to attend the daily Bible lesson held each morning after breakfast. Even the preacher and his wife had to attend it,

Brother Harley's orders. They also had to attend four of the seven Christian services held one a night after the evening meal. Local pastors came out, often bringing with them some of their congregation. When they brought musicians, they went over very well.

Time fled. The first winter snow caught them by surprise. Hobbit warned that they would have to be getting over the Rockies pretty soon. Little Debbie and Mary the woman had been working in the Mission's thrift store sorting clothes that were donated, so they had already put together five bedrolls plus warm clothes for all six of them. Screaming Girl helped to keep the Homeless Emergency Shelter clean, and did a little cleaning in the children's quarters. She learned that there were seventeen children, all of who had been abandoned somewhere in the state of Utah. Of the seventeen, six were boys, eleven girls. They were all adorable to the point that she wished she could stay with them. After talking with California Red and learning that two male cooks had came in out of the cold, Hobbit told the five to start making plans for figuring on the best time to tell Bertha that they were leaving. They didn't want anyone to have any hard feelings toward them.

Hobbit got the southbound freight schedule from one of the yardmen in the Helper freight yard. When he went across the road to get a two-pound canned ham, a small jar of mustard, and a large jar of instant coffee, he paid cash for the items. He just as easily could have shoplifted the items, but Helper was too small a town. They would miss the items, remember him, and it would give the Mission a bad name. My heck, he thought, it doesn't matter if they understood God or not; they still help people, especially those kids.

Mentally, he made plans to leave that weekend.

After talking to Bertha and thanking her, the six said goodbye to the others. On Saturday morning at six o'clock, they caught a freight headed for Grand Junction, Colorado. The six would look things over in Grand Junction and, if the snow didn't look too bad in the Rockies, they would continue straight on to Denver. Once they got east of Denver things would be a little warmer.

The population of Grand Junction is ten times that of Helper, and three times that of the whole Price-Helper area. Hobbit considered it during the trip, giving him something to think about. At least he wouldn't have to give up his favorite pastime because of the bad image it would make.

At Grand Junction, they learned that the mountains were clear of snow downfall, but it was below zero at the top and below freezing in Denver. They all voted to continue. At some time or another they had all crossed the Rockies during the snows.

Before they began unloading from the boxcar, California Red and Little Debbie went toward the freight offices to check on the time the train would leave for Denver. When they returned, Red told the others, "It'll be three hours, and we will have to find another empty on the train making up on track nine."

"Well," Hobbit responded, "Did you fix your watches with the railroad's time clock?" California Red admitted that they hadn't.

"It won't do any good for us to synchronize ours," Hobbit continued. "So let's all of us take a look at them now, and figure to meet back here in two hours."

Everybody agreed. All went off in pairs, looking at their watches. Hobbit and Mary the woman returned with smiles on their faces. The other four were already there.

Jack Frost spoke up, "Hobbit, Screaming Girl and I got here a little early and we checked: there's not a single empty on the train making up on track nine."

The big Polack scratched his head momentarily, then told them, "You'll have to walk the train again and find a car that doesn't have a seal on the door. We can open it without making anybody mad, and it will be empty."

Hobbit and Mary the woman went to the outer edges of the freight yard to find something to open the door with. After a while, they came upon a piece of track about four feet long. Each picking up an end, they headed for the train. The boxcar doors operated on a track in the floor. On the outside, there is a lever that is pushed down into a brace. If the lever has a seal in it, it is a federal crime to break the seal. But even with no seal on it, the door lever has to be knocked up with something heavy in order to get it open.

The travelers were running late, and it was Jack Frost who gave the hobo call again, then rapped three times for hurry up.

California Red and Little Debbie had gone in an opposite direction from Jack Frost and Screaming Girl and they started running toward the call. As they came upon Hobbit and Mary the woman, they relieved them of the piece of track and continued to trot towards Jack Frost. Hobbit walked briskly, but didn't run. By the time he and Mary the woman got to the car, the others had it open and were loading up their packs and bedrolls. They put everything in the front of the boxcar closest to the engine. That would keep the wind from making direct contact with them. You could not close the doors. You would be locked in and there would be a long time before you were found—dead or alive.

The train would not run very fast going up the mountain, slow, as a matter of fact, but going down it would pour it on. That would make it really cold.

After the train moved out of the Grand Junction yard, it wasn't long before it was rolling up the western foothills of the great Rocky Mountains, beginning its hundred mile ascent which would crest at almost two miles above sea level.

Hobbit nodded to Mary the woman, and she reached into her pack producing a fifth of Thunderbird. They had both done well during the two hours they walked the streets of Grand Junction, and they were proud to share their success with the others. After taking a drink, she passed the bottle on, starting a pack of cigarettes in the same direction.

She decided that they would save the food until later, when they went down the mountain.

After they had smoked, they began nodding out, resting from being tired, anesthetized by the wine.

They all began waking from the cold, and Screaming Girl checked her watch, commenting, "It's been three hours. We must be at the top of the hump."

Everyone agreed. The cold had reached their bones.

Both Mary the woman and Hobbit began pulling food out of their packs, then another bottle of Thunderbird. When the sandwiches were made and all began eating, Hobbit brought out another jug of Thunderbird, taking a drink himself, then passing it around.

It was going to be cold as a well digger's behind going down that mountain, Hobbit thought to himself. They had better get ready for it.

Everyone had put on extra socks, jogging pants and sweatshirts. They climbed into their bedrolls, pulling shower curtains over them. Hobbit produced two more bottles of Thunderbird, he and Mary the woman dwelling on one of them for a while. Hearing that the others were going to spend some time making small talk and idle conversation, Mary the woman handed out two more packs of cigarettes. Hobbit slipped off into dreamland, only half asleep, reliving his youth.

He had been born June 18, 1957, the first child of Brooke Eugene and Sadie Mae Horseman. They named him Junior after his father.

At the age of five months, he developed an infection in the mastoid of his right ear. The resulting surgery left him deaf there. By the time he was two years old, he began his criminal career: he toddled away from home and was found in the parking lot of the old Sears-Roebuck store. For that escapade, he was labeled a run-a-way.

By the time he was eight years old, the juvenile court made a special reform school out of the state orphanage to put him in for being incorrigible to his parents.

At age ten, he was sent to the state industrial school, a prison for children who had not committed a crime, but were a nuisance to society.

When he was fifteen years old, he ran away from the industrial school and committed his first crime. He was charged with and later pleaded guilty to assault with intent to kill. Because he was a prisoner of the industrial school, and because the officials there didn't want him back, he was sent to the state penitentiary where he was held as a safekeeper on death row.

Five months of such treatment would drive an ordinary boy insane. Not so Brooke Eugene Horseman, Jr. He became meaner and meaner. Not cleverer, however, and that resulted in another prison term.

During his last prison term, he had finished high school and, when he was released, he enrolled in the University of South Carolina.

After becoming disillusioned with the system he quit college, going first to Atlanta, Georgia, where he became a political activist. Again, not finding what he wanted, he returned to crime, but this time as a hobo.

He had hoboed all over the continental United States, stealing and learning to steal, teaching others how to steal, and sometimes causing the rules of crime to be changed. Now, the time of his wine had come. He was about to make a great effort to get off the road and begin living like a human being again.

Sleep finally overcame him, and he awakened to the sound of Mary the woman telling him they were in Denver. She had shaken him a little, too.

Bright and refreshed from two sleeps, Hobbit began giving instructions.

"One of you volunteer to go find out when the next train leaves, headed east. We will get your pack and bedroll together. Now we are headed to Salina, Kansas. At Salina we will turn south."

Nobody offered to volunteer, so Mary the woman said she would go. As Hobbit began putting her pack together he felt two bottles and spied them for Thunderbird. She did better than I did, he thought.

Mary the woman had no longer been gone until she came back, running at a fast trot. "We have to get out of here!" she exclaimed. "This is a hot yard. They had some kind of trouble, and the police are arresting everyone they see in the yard."

She didn't have to explain. At her first exclamation, the others had begun snatching up their packs and bedrolls. As they hurried out of the rail yard, they began saying "Shoot."

Hobbit said "Shoot" a few times and then switched to a four-letter word.

"What are we going to do now, Hobbit?" Screaming Girl asked with much concern.

"Let's get out of this yard first," he answered. "Then we will figure our options. Times like this are not good times to start making decisions. First thing you know you've made a mistake and everything falls apart."

When they had cleared the freight yard they slowed down, but didn't stop. Hobbit was thinking. He still had quite a lot of money from the restaurant, and now would be a good time to spend some of it.

As he walked, he checked out the signs on the buildings until he spotted one that said "Rooms for rent." Couldn't have asked for anything better, he thought to himself. This was a cheap district and "Rooms for rent" always meant that the room was cheaper than a hotel, even a flop. Turning toward the sign, he led the rest of them. When he was almost in front of the building, he motioned for the others to wait. They leaned back against the wall of a building while Hobbit went in to rent the room. He did real well. For only seven dollars and a half he obtained a room, and the bath and toilet were not far down the hall.

When he had finished putting his things away in the room, he went down the hall to find the fire escape. Finding it, he tried the door. It opened easily. The desk man downstairs hadn't seemed like he was interested in anything except the t-v he was watching, so Hobbit didn't anticipate any problem with him when he got the others sneaked in.

After descending the fire escape, he walked around the block and waved the others to come on. They walked quietly to the fire escape, then softly up the steps. In the room, they spoke just above a whisper, because, even if the desk man didn't care, anyone who got mad at you for making too much noise could turn you in to the police for sleeping six people in a one-person occupancy room.

The first thing they decided was that the women would take their baths first. If they ran out of hot water it would be acceptable for the men to smell and be a little dirty, not so the women. The next decision mandated that the men would all get empty half gallon milk jugs to use during the night, plus a couple of number ten cans just in case another roomer had to use the toilet and one of the women couldn't hold it. Finally, the subject turned to food. That was when Hobbit revealed that he had cracked the safe in the restaurant and had gotten quite a bit of money. How much, he didn't know. He had never bothered to count it.

They all wanted steaks.

Hobbit could just see his money disappearing into the hands of a cashier. But he knew he had to do it. The police might spot them for tramps and arrest them even if they weren't in the freight yard.

Looking their best, they went down the fire escape, heading toward the nicer part of town. When they arrived in front of the Rattlesnake Inn, Hobbit figured it would be a reasonable place to eat. Leading the others to the inside entrance, he waited until a waiter ushered them to a table, and asked if there would be anything before they ordered. They all said "coffee."

After they had finished their coffee, the waiter returned and took their order. All of them selected a salad, ribeye steak, baked potato, and green beans. The women were enthralled. Screaming Girl enhanced their mood with the knowledge that the place was owned by one of the great chefs of the west. Hobbit heard this and tried to recall the prices on the menu. He couldn't, but when another waiter came by with menus he asked for one. There were no prices on the menu. He flinched a little but said nothing, devoting some time to think about the matter. When they had finished the main course, they ordered dessert. Hobbit watched them until they had almost finished, then told them, "Ya'll go on ahead and I'll catch up with you."

As soon as they had all finished, they left. When the waiter came by again Hobbit ordered another cup of coffee and separate checks. The waiter knew he'd been had and he also knew that there wasn't anything he could do about it. Returning, he brought coffee and six individual checks. Finishing his coffee, Hobbit walked to the cashier booth and paid his bill.

The others were in the rented room when he returned. Mary had her last bottle of wine out, but had waited until Hobbit returned to open it. He had one left also, and retrieved it from his pack. After a while, they were talking too loudly, but discovered that a man down the hall had his t-v going wide open; they didn't pay noise any more attention.

They woke early the next morning, and, smelling someone down the hall making coffee, they brewed up a pot of their own.

It would be a while before checkout time. They needed to talk about the problem. After discarding the plastic milk containers and number ten cans, they sat down to do some serious talking.

The first thing they discounted was hitch hiking. Even if someone should pick up a crowd of six people, they would let them out at the next exit, even if they had to exit off themselves. Hobbit discounted the bus. He had enough money for the bus, but they were going to need that money when they got to Florida.

No one wanted to steal a car: too much risk for too little whatever. Finally, they decided to lighten their packs and bedrolls and catch a train on the fly as it went out of town. All trains had to go very slowly while in town, never more than fifteen miles an hour in busy districts. So they would go out to the eastern side of the freight yard and follow the tracks out until a slow freight came along. They knew that they would probably have to catch a piggyback, but it would soon be warmer across Kansas and they believed that they could make it. Decided, they went down the fire escape out to the freight yard.

When they were within a block of the freight yard, Little Debbie, who was leading the group, jumped back against a brick wall. She told them that a city police car was sitting next to the tracks with two officers in it.

The restaurant, thought Hobbit. It had to be the restaurant.

As they headed up the eastbound street with Screaming Girl now in the lead, Hobbit told them what he had done at the restaurant. They stepped up the pace almost to a run.

Finally, California Red touched Screaming Girl, motioning to the right, and, at the next intersection, she turned. Slowing down, they walked closer to the freight yard, and were pleased when they discovered that they were on the eastern end. They looked, but could not see the police car.

Without getting back on railroad property, they made their way out to where the tracks began dividing. There, picking a track headed due east, they began walking leisurely, waiting for the warning sound of an oncoming freight. But when they found a high spot of ground next to the tracks, they stopped, planning to wait there for a freight train going east. The high ground would give them an edge on catching the train.

Hobbit had caught many trains on the fly, and he was sure that Mary the woman had, also, but he wasn't sure about the others. They were all game, maybe a little too much so, and it might be hard to get the truth out of them concerning how many trains they had caught while running at breakneck speed. So he didn't ask. When the train rounded the bend in the street and came into full sight, they were elated. There were only two engines, which meant they were definitely headed across the flatlands of western Kansas, and there were a number of empties and several piggybacks.

The first empties that came by had their doors half shut. Hobbit didn't want to risk it. If you miss hanging a freight on the run you are risking being thrown back into the tracks and under the cold steel wheels of the train.

Finally, as the train shortened, the women moved in front of the men, preparing to hop a piggyback. Piggybacks are flat cars that got their names from transporting freight in trailers that are ordinarily used by truckers for over-the-road hauling. Usually, each piggyback has two trailers. Since the trailers are on wheels, and the wheels on tires, there is ample space for travelers underneath them. On the outside of both ends of the flat cars, a set of three small, flat stepping rungs provided a means of walking up to the car. Catching it on the fly, as it is called, requires the hopeful hobo to first throw onto the flat car everything he is carrying, then mount the car at the last set of rungs. This also is dangerous.

All of the six travelers began running beside the train. When the car in front of the piggyback approached, the men began running along side the train followed by the women. The men threw their packs and rolls on first, then helped the women throw theirs on. When everything was on, the women began mounting the rear rungs by grasping a trailer hold-down and being thrown onto the flat top by one of the men. After all of the women were on board, Hobbit jumped on and helped the other two men to mount in the same fashion. As long as you don't jump too far there is less danger in this method.

Slowly, they crawled under the trailers and headed to the front of the flat car. At the front, they pulled out their shower curtains and wrapped them on their backs to block the cold wind. Then they paired off and sat in two file rows. Every once in a while, the three in the back would swap with the three in the front, and this routine continued until they reached Salina, Kansas. There they caught an empty headed south to Wichita. In Wichita, the six travelers, tired, weary, hungry, and needing a drink, decided to hold up for a while. Although Hobbit usually didn't drink, he said he would buy a bottle of Thunderbird and have a drink or two out of it himself. He knew better than to buy more than that because they would all get drunk. He didn't blame them for drinking. Their problems were just different from his.

While they were walking up the street, looking for a place to buy the Thunderbird, they saw a large supermarket and the conversation picked up about shoplifting.

Ordinarily, Hobbit would not have approved, but he had enough money to pay for anything they were caught with, so he told them to go ahead. He was too tired, he told them, and would wait outside.

They were all smiles when they came out. No problems, they said, and headed back to the freight yard.

The food was revitalizing. It made the weary Polack sleepy, but he maintained his consciousness and asked, "How about the Thunderbird?"

All five smiled and each withdrew a fifth of Thunderbird. They had one-upped on him and scraped the label off the bottles. The electric eye had to have the label to activate its sensor.

Hobbit smiled. It was just a queer kind of luck that he was able to get this bunch. They didn't make many like them.

"Look," he spoke humbly, "I know that all of you have earned a good drunk; but let's get our thinker on. We need to catch a train out of here pretty soon, and you sure can't do it drunk. So how about letting me hold all but one bottle of your wine for you."

They didn't look at each other at first. This was a very serious matter. But when they did look, they were all in agreement: they would give Hobbit the wine. In the meantime, California Red opened his bottle while the others gave theirs up.

Propping himself up against the building facing the rail yard, Hobbit slipped off into dreamland again. When he woke, he knew he had been dreaming, but couldn't recall what it was about. The others, too, had fallen asleep, so, slipping his bag and bedroll back into the shadows, he started toward the freight yard to find out when and where was the next train headed south. Experienced trainmen would always tell you. The young ones wouldn't and might even call the railroad special agent. Experienced hobos always avoided the young ones.

The next freight train going south was leaving at six in the morning on the third set of rails from the eastside of the yard tower. That would give them plenty of time to find an empty boxcar.

When he started back, he noticed that the other five travelers were up milling around, probably looking for his pack with the wine in it, he thought.

"Train doesn't leave until six in the morning, so we have plenty of time to have another Thunderbird and look for an empty," Hobbit told them.

A train was already being made up on track three. Jack Frost walked over to the yardman to find out if it was the one going south at six in the morning. He had gotten on the wrong train a time or two until he learned to ask about the one they were making up. The yardman verified that it was the train, and Jack Frost returned to tell the others.

When they found an empty boxcar, they checked it to see how clean it was. As much time as they had, they could be choosy. All agreed that this one would be alright and they all boarded. While boarding, they learned that the car was padded, making it easier to sleep in.

They shared another bottle of Thunderbird, and, after several cigarettes and some conversation, fell asleep.

They wakened to the jar of boxcars being humped to another train. Looking out, none of them recognized the rail yard and none of them knew where they were. Jack Frost volunteered to try and find out, asking the others to throw his gear off if the train began moving out. Screaming Girl assured him that she would jump off with his gear and the others seconded her.

When he returned, Jack Frost was shaking his head as if still in amazement. "We're in Fort Worth, Texas," he told them. "And we still have to go through Dallas to get out of here. We have to be real careful when we leave Dallas because we could end up in Texarkana just as well as we could Shreveport. I told them where we were headed and they were really helpful."

Mary the woman spoke up, "How about laying over in Dallas? I know somebody there and they wouldn't mind having us for two or three days."

Hobbit said he thought it was a good idea, and the others agreed.

Jack Frost had made sure that the car they were in was going on to Dallas, but could not determine if it was going farther. He was told to ask about a southeast bound train in Dallas because there was no way of telling anything in Fort Worth.

But the train didn't stop in Dallas. It highballed straight through.

Luck was with them. They arrived in Shreveport, Louisiana, in the wee hours of the next day and all were glad to find that the train was breaking up. They had not been able to sleep because of bad track and they needed the stop in order to rest.

Before they realized it, they felt the car they were on being humped. Quickly, they grabbed their gear and jumped off the train. When a humped car locks in with another, it has a hard jar and anyone in either car can be hurt seriously. Scattered down the lane between the tracks, the six travelers were trying to get together when a beam of a spotlight fell on them. It was a hot yard and that was a policeman. A voice from a loud speaker in a police car told them to lay on the ground and put their hands behind their backs. They complied, knowing that the officer was calling for back up. When the backup came, they were taken to jail.

The first thing the jailer was told about them was that the big Polack had a bag full of change in his pack. This caused the jailer to search him and he found the bills also.

Suspicious of Hobbit, the jailer put him in a cell by himself. Not being a smoker or a drinker, he didn't mind the jail or the discovery of the money. All that would take care of itself.

The two police officers who had arrested them at the freight yard went to Hobbit's cell and asked if he wanted to cooperate. He asked them "About what?" and they told him "About the money you had in your pack." He told them he wanted a lawyer. They left.

When the six travelers went before the municipal court judge the next morning, the presiding judge asked the two officers if they had anything to say. The first one explained that he had observed the people jumping out of a moving boxcar and that it appeared they had hurt themselves. He put his spotlight on them and called for backup. The second officer stated that he had assisted in transporting the people to jail. He also added that Horseman had an unusual amount of change, plus one and five dollar bills. He told the judge that when Horseman was asked about the money, he requested a lawyer. In view of these circumstances, the officer added, it was the desire of the police department to hold the man for at least a week in order for them to do some further checking on him.

The judge sentenced all six of them to ten days in jail.

The jailer assigned the three men to one cell and the three women to another. He put all of them to cleaning up the run-around outside the cells.

Fortunately for those who smoked, Hobbit had gotten by with twenty five-dollar bills he had kept in the cloth lining inside his shoes. As soon as they met in the run-around he gave Mary the woman twenty dollars with which to buy cigarettes. He gave California Red the money to get a carton for himself and Jack Frost.

The next day California Red came to Hobbit with a fist full of dollar bills and a handful of change. When asked where he got the money, he said he had sold eight packs of cigarettes for three dollars a pack. Explaining, he told Hobbit that the people in the cells had money but no way to send out a trusty for things they wanted to buy. Since they did have a way to do that, they could get themselves a lucrative business going—and they did. Pretty soon, with the help of a trusty, they had a very profitable jailhouse hustle.

Fate wouldn't have it but that the women got the trusty to bring them in a fifth of Thunderbird. When they got to making too much noise, the jailer went to their cell, smelled the wine and, searching, found the empty bottle. Asked where they got the wine, they all said they wanted a lawyer.

The jailer put the women back on lock down, but left the men out. He also forbade the trusty to have anything to do with any other prisoners unless he told him to.

The police failed to find out anything more about Hobbit, and at the end of the ten days all six of the travelers were released from jail; the money returned to Hobbit. Rested but nerve-draggled, they headed for the nearest liquor store.

All six of them had made money during their short venture with jail finances, so each of them felt a sense of individual independence. At the liquor store they asserted this, and bought some of the best whiskey in the store. When they left, the five drinkers were well loaded down with Jack Daniels, Crown Royal, and Four Roses. Hobbit had bought a half a pint of cheap vodka. The others were broke, and if they didn't kill themselves or get arrested again, they would need a drink when they started sobering up. He had learned a long time ago that it is a very aggravating experience to be around a drunk unless you are drunk, too; so he walked down to the freight yard, figuring he could find them in the morning. They wouldn't go far from where they bought the whiskey.

Sure enough, the next morning about nine o'clock he found them in an alley behind a dumpster, their packs and bed rolls intact, but all a little worse for the drinking. He let all of them get a drink of the vodka, which killed it, then told them to get their gear together and led them down to the freight yard. They wouldn't be hungry for a while, but they would be thirsty. He had an empty plastic gallon jug in his pack, so this he took to the train yard and filled it with water. When he got back to the group he told them that they had two hours until the train left. He, in the meantime, would buy

cigarettes for them if they needed some. They did, so he left to find a place to eat breakfast, then to buy the cigarettes. When he returned, it was time to find an empty. He had already asked about the time and the line, and they soon left the Shreveport yard headed for Alexandria.

When they arrived at the freight yard in Alexandria, Louisiana, they could hear the noise of other cars being humped and straightway got their stuff together and got out of the yard. Ten days in jail had been enough for not doing anything.

Hobbit told them that they would come back later and catch a freight to Baton Rouge, then on to Alabama and Florida. Screaming Girl screamed. She had never been in New Orleans, and this might be her last chance ever, and, if she couldn't go to New Orleans with them, she would go without them. There was no use in arguing with her, so the schedule was changed: first to Baton Rouge; then south to New Orleans. But the big Polack made one condition: they do all of their shopping in Baton Rouge. New Orleans was too hot a town to do any shoplifting in, and they would certainly need new clothes and stuff to walk around and see the sights without being arrested.

Everyone agreed, and Mary the woman asked Hobbit if he was going to get new clothes. He told her "yes." He never wanted to be different from them; he just was. He had a problem, but his was different from theirs. He wanted to get out of the social prison he was in, and he had a passion for getting out right away. But things can wait, he told himself. Things can wait.

Alexandria proved to be a larger town than they had thought. Like many other cities, the town had expanded and had built subdivisions with shopping centers. When Jack Frost saw the leather dress jacket in the K-Mart show window, he spoke up immediately, saying, "I'm going to do my shopping right here."

The others chimed in and Hobbit said "Oh, what the heck." He would dress out there, too.

A problem arose. They all had field jackets and mountain boots; ideal for hoboing, not good for sneaking out of a store with new dress clothes on. Several solutions were suggested—leaving their coats and going in one at a time, going barefooted, or having the men leave their shoes in the wastebasket in the women's rest room and let the women go in behind them to lift a big shoulder strap purse and put the shoes in it. None of these would work. The best one would only work for Jack Frost. Both Hobbit and California Red wore size fourteen-and-a-half shoes, too big to fit into a purse.

Little Debbie had been listening and had figured the thing out. "OK," she told them. "Listen up. We will go in one at a time, leaving our jackets to be watched by the others. Now, I know you are accustomed to leaving all of your clothes in the restroom trashcan, but we will do it differently this time. We will just bring them, the jackets and the shoes out with us."

"How are we going to do that?" Mary the woman demanded.

"We will search the parking lot for K-Mart shopping bags and put the stuff in them", replied Red. "There's something wrong with that plan," Hobbit broke in. "If we are going to bring the old stuff out in shopping bags, why don't we just take the labels off the new stuff and put them in the bags?"

Little Debbie looked at him like she could slit his throat, but she neither did nor said anything.

"Let's stick to leaving the coats out here and work on the shoes," Hobbit said in an authoritative voice.

Everyone remained silent. No one spoke for several minutes. All were afraid of the embarrassment of coming up with an idea that had holes in it.

Finally, Little Debbie spoke up again. " I think I've got it," she told them. "We won't get dress clothes here. We'll get socks, underwear, shirts and blue jeans. We can wear our jackets and boots in, discard our shirts, pants, and underclothes; then wear our jackets and boots out with the new work clothes. Afterwards, we can go to Wal-Mart. At Wal-Mart we can get dress shoes and we women can sneak them out in our purses. We can leave Hobbit's and Red's shoes in the trash can inside, then go back and bring out one shoe at a time. We can get our dress clothes in Baton Rouge, like Hobbit tried to tell us to start with."

Things went well at K-Mart, but Jack Frost didn't get his leather jacket. He really didn't want to be that different, anyway. At Wal-Mart, everything went as planned. They obtained work clothes and shirts, California Red getting shoe polish for their boots. The ride to Baton Rouge would be short, not long enough to get their clothes dirty, and they could do some more serious shopping there. They would arrive in New Orleans in style!

Baton Rouge proved to be a city of excitement for the women, and at their insistence, along with a little prodding from California Red, they decided to stay in the city and sight-see for a couple of days.

The old southern capital city was a sight to behold. Its own mightiness was dwarfed by the flow of the great Mississippi River on whose banks the city was built. None of the women had ever before seen so great a river. It was almost a sin to shoplift in a city like this, but it had to be done; Hobbit was right, they had heard about the notoriety of the New Orleans police.

Hobbit went over the finer points of contemporary shoplifting. He explained that they could not search you, but they could search a bag inside the store or outside if it set the electronic alarm off. The thing to do, he suggested, was to go to a lot of different stores and get only one item each from each store. By removing the label and the price tag, the item could not set off the electronic alarm, and one item could be hidden on one's person without arousing suspicion. The system worked. All of the travelers soon had a small wardrobe.

Hobbit paid for a room down near the freight yard. The women obtained food in the usual manner. No one questioned why they did not get new boots. The boots they had—shoplifted, too—were very expensive.

The next day the women, along with California Red, went sightseeing. Hobbit and Jack Frost went over to the rail yard to check on trains going to New Orleans. Because the women and California Red were not back at check out time, Hobbit paid for another day.

When the four interlopers returned, they had gifts for Hobbit and Jack Frost: a whole baked chicken and a small bag of mini bottles of whiskey. They also had a small, black puppy, which they had named Gerterka. Each of them had taken two letters each and the name came out that way.

Everyone liked the little pup, and it was soon spoiled rotten.

Jack Frost and Hobbit had found out that a train bound for New Orleans would start making up shortly after midnight, and would probably be pulling out at around three-thirty in the morning. It would make up on track nine.

Little Debbie drew the first watch after midnight. She sat outside where she could watch the tracks, wondering what it would be like to get off the road. Nearly three years had gone by since she walked out to the freight yards in Ogden, Utah. She had no family she could go back to. Her child had been taken away from her by court order. Her husband had divorced her. She knew she would have to stop drinking, no matter how much money they got. All the money in Fort Knox wouldn't buy off an alcohol habit, and the alcohol habit could cost you everything. Tears rolled down her cheeks as she thought of what she had already lost.

The train started making up just after twelve thirty.

None of the boxcars had doors open on the side Little Debbie was watching from. She decided to call the next watcher, because it was too early to have to go to the other side of the train to hunt an open boxcar.

Screaming Girl was next. Her shift was uneventful, also.

When Mary the woman was about a half an hour into her shift, an empty boxcar was connected to the line of others. She walked over to the tracks to check it out. It was fine. Not cushioned, but very clean. She walked back to wake the five.

Soon, the six travelers, their packs full of new clothes and shoes, and the women with new shoulder strap handbags, headed toward the empty freight car on track nine. Once the train got underway it wouldn't be long before they would be in New Orleans. Nevertheless, they all went back to sleep.

Hobbit didn't exactly know where the Rescue Mission was in New Orleans, but he had the address along with the knowledge of what he had been told. Three free nights, he had been told. That ought to satisfy the women. But it worried him some, about their drinking, getting pie-eyed drunk. They couldn't do that in New Orleans except during Mardi Gras. Otherwise, you had to have money for a cab and an address for the cabbie to take you to. Then, too, the Mission wouldn't let you come in if you had been drinking.

When they arrived in New Orleans it was still morning and there was little need of going to the Mission before mid-afternoon, so they headed for the bus station and put their gear in lockers there. They asked someone in the bus station for directions to the French Quarter and were directed to Bourbon Street. It was too early for Bourbon Street, so they walked over to St. Charles and found an inexpensive place to have breakfast. Finishing there, they walked back to the French Quarter district, the women gasping at the beauty of the buildings, the courtyards, and the almost affectionate politeness of the people. They would easily spend three days here.

Later that afternoon, they went to the Mission where they checked in for three days. The Mission, an International Mission member, had a regular check-in time as do all International Missions. Each person using the shelter must attend the afternoon Christian services. Immediately after services, the evening meal is served. After the meal, shower and to bed. The only way to get around the "shower to bed" thing was to slip out after the lights were out at bedtime. Except for the resident staff, no one was allowed in the Mission after breakfast. This is not true of all Missions. Some hold a morning service at around ten o'clock and a meal at eleven. All are welcome.

The travelers headed back to the French Quarter. The women were already enthralled with the little they had seen of it. They saw beauty everywhere. The ornamental balustrades almost made them swoon, and the elegant courtyards of flowers and shrubs elicited cries of ecstasy from them. The men commented on the quaintness of the architecture and found the locations of the places of entertainment interesting.

Hobbit offered to buy everyone a sandwich and coke for lunch; all accepted. After lunch, he suggested that they go look around New Orleans and come back to the French Quarter that night. He told them that he would check the Mission out and find a way to sneak out. After all, it was a Mission, not a jail.

They had left their packs and bedrolls back at the Mission; walking light gave them extra energy to make better time. They didn't gawk too much after they left the French Quarter, although they did have to stop as someone would see something particularly appealing in a storefront window. It seemed as if New Orleans was designed to be enjoyed.

As they neared the northern part of New Orleans, Hobbit began slowing down, watching people. They knew he was looking for something in particular, but he didn't say so they didn't ask. Soon, however, he steered them into an alleyway and told them that just down and across the street a Cajun was selling dope. He told them he wanted them to all get a good look at him.

They didn't stare. They knew better than that; but as they walked down the street, they all made furtive glances in his direction. The Cajun was a big man. He had a powerful build and a mean look. They all said later that they wouldn't want to run up on him in a dark alley at night.

Jack Frost commented independently that he wouldn't want to run up on him anytime, anywhere.

In a little while, they turned northeast and soon came upon a huge shopping center. Hobbit had made strict rules against any kind of lifting stuff in New Orleans. But one could dream, couldn't one?

When they all returned to the Mission that evening, they got their gear from the safe room, and Hobbit checked his pack to see if the coins were still there. They were. He had put the bills in his front pocket and he had thought of changing the silver to bills; but he cringed at the idea of having to take that much change to the bank. It gave him the jitters.

The Mission cook had agreed to feed and water the puppy, Gerterka.

The evening meal at the Mission was pretty good, and the Christian service hadn't been so bad, either. Two young women played guitars and sang some Christian songs; then a man preached for a while. He really did put on a show at the end, almost begging people to come forward. Jack Frost started to go up there just to make the fellow feel better, but he thought better of it since he and the others were going to sneak out later. Getting caught having sneaked out was tantamount to a major sin, and most Missions would expel you for doing it. They had many and varied reasons for doing that, the main one being that each person had signed an agreement that he or she would remain in the Mission until the wake-up call in the morning.

When he had taken his shower, Hobbit moved about on the men's dormitory floor, finally figuring a way out and in. This still left finding a way to get the women off the floor above them. His plan now was to get out on the fire escape, then go up and into the women's dorm from there. He had told Mary the woman to watch out for him about an hour after the lights were turned out. When it was time, he headed for the bathroom where a window led to the fire escape. He had to be extra careful reaching over to the fire escape, because it was a two-story drop from where he was to the hard pavement down below.

Pulling himself up the fire escape, he quickly made his way up to the next floor. The bathroom window was in the same place on this floor as it was on the men's, and he had a problem getting from the fire escape to the window. This accomplished, however, he spotted a woman rinsing her face and tapped the window, believing it was Mary the woman. It wasn't. The woman ran out of the bathroom screaming so it put

Screaming Girl to shame, and he could hear someone say "Call downstairs for the night watchman!"

Instead of pulling himself over to the fire escape, he leaped, almost pushing his foot off the brick ridge under the bathroom window. He proceeded much more cautiously when he went from the fire escape to the window in the men's bathroom. As soon as he got to his bed, he took his clothes off, rolled them up and put them under his pillow; then he got into bed under the covers. Perhaps the three women would be able to explain to the woman what had happened, and she wouldn't identify him at breakfast the next morning. Nevertheless, he approached breakfast with much tribulation, and only after no one screamed when he sat down to the table did he feel safe.

There was no early morning service, so, after checking their gear into the safe room, they headed out on the town.

The women had calmed the woman down; they told her who she had seen and why. She said it was alright, it was just that she had been raped so many times that she couldn't take being raped in the Mission. Hers was the typical story of an alcoholic woman on the road or in the streets, and the three women understood completely.

With Hobbit's fears and apprehension abated, they began discussing the events of the night before as they lollygagged down the street. First of all, they all agreed that they had needed the rest and sleep they had gotten. Second of all, the women and Jack Frost were apprehensive about going in and out the window to the fire escape. It wasn't too hard for the two tall men, but for the rest of them, the reach might be too far, and it was a long drop to the street.

Finally, Little Debbie suggested that they rest and sleep in the Mission every night and see the city during the day; then sleep out for a night or two in order to see Bourbon Street and the rest of the French Quarter at night. The idea sounded good and they agreed on it. They would spend this day and the next seeing the town in the daytime. They would go down to the bus station and leave their gear in lockers, and afterwards find a place where they could sit around most of the time, being sure they would be in good shape for Bourbon Street when the time came.

About two hours before time to be in at the Mission, Hobbit asked them to head back through the same route they had taken out the day before. He wanted to have another look at the Cajun.

The big Cajun had a good business. From the point where you could see him and tell what he was doing until you passed him, he would have made at least one sale. That was pretty good. At ten dollars a hit, he was taking in a minimum of a hundred and twenty dollars an hour. And, every once in a while, he would make a big sale of three hundred dollars or more; probably pulling from fifteen hundred to two thousand dollars a day, half of which was profit. Who else makes forty to fifty thousand dollars a year for standing on the street passing out little packets of white stuff and taking in good ol' yum drool cash yankee dollars.

"What are you thinking?" California Red asked him.

"I'm thinking," he answered.

"Does it include us?" Red questioned.

"Yes," he said.

At that point all of them began chiming in with questions, statements, and general dissertations on the matter.

Finally, Hobbit told them. He wanted to get a can of aerosol ether tomorrow, and, before they left New Orleans, he wanted to rob the big Cajun drug dealer.

They had all been silent for a while before Screaming Girl spoke up, saying, "Jack Frost and I will have to think about that. Besides, he's one of us. We're all trimixes, same as that Cajun. All of the women are, anyway.

"Hobbit didn't mean to offend anybody," said Jack Frost, speaking to everyone. "He sees a need for money and that Cajun drug dealer is the best bet. Now, we all agreed to follow Hobbit. This is not a good time to back out."

Everyone remained quiet until Screaming Girl broke the silence, saying, "I'll let you know in the morning."

Hobbit was not disappointed. As much as was his need for cash, his need for a show of trust by the others was even greater. It was important to find out now. At this point he could still turn around, and perhaps find replacements for each of them, but not later when he began implementing the big score. Happily, in the morning Screaming Girl was in good spirits, and said, "Yes," she would go with Hobbit.

But Hobbit kept it in mind. He would look for signs.

With that matter settled, all of them joined in on planning the job. That night would be their last night at the Mission; consequently, they would have to have a working plan before the end of the day.

Instead of walking out on the town again, Mary the woman suggested that they tour the French Quarter. Everyone agreed.

This time they stopped and peered into windows, appraising the things inside with authoritative insight—except for the things they had never seen before. These drew various statements made in many different octaves.

For lunch, they stopped at Diamond Jim's restaurant. Hobbit had put ten rolls of quarters in his pocket, and he would use them to pay.

Reading from the menu, all of them ordered something different from the others. It was a good sign, Hobbit thought to himself. They were acting independently now, and all of them were on his side. So far the plan was working out real well.

The woman at the cash register took Hobbit's money without remark. It had been cheaper than he thought it would be. Maybe enough left for a drink.

"What do you all say to having a drink before going in tonight?" he asked them.

There was a wild shout of expectation from the five alcoholics. They hadn't had a drink for over two days.

The Christian service at the Mission was pretty good that night. One of the women who came could play the Mission's piano, and that made the singing meaningful. Many of the songs they sang the travelers had heard in other missions; but a few were new and that added something of interest to the service.

Drugs and alcohol were preached on that night. It was one of those toe-stepping-on sermons: if you used drugs or drank alcohol you felt a little pain somewhere. All of the travelers were affected by the sermon, and, before the evening meal was over, California Red remarked, "A few more like that and I'd quit."

The rest of the night went by uneventfully.

When they were awakened at day break, they got all of their gear together, ate breakfast at the Mission, then headed to the bus station where they would put their packs and bed rolls in lockers for safe keeping during the day. They had discussed having the Mission laundry man wash and dry their dirty clothes—he would do it for two or three dollars, depending on how much dirty clothes you had—but they decided against it because they knew they might not be able to get back to the Mission after ripping off the big Cajun drug dealer. They might even be lucky to get back to the bus station.

After they had stashed their gear in the bus station lockers, they went for a stroll down to Canal Street. At the western end of the street, they took a ferry across the Mississippi River just to say they had done it.

After coming back from the river, they continued their stroll, going out the other side of the street this time. Several blocks down, Jack Frost exclaimed again—the way he had when he had seen the first leather coat. This one was particularly beautiful. Hand tooled and laced with leather at all the hems, it was elegant.

"I'm going to have to have that coat," Jack Frost announced to everyone. "It's too beautiful to pass up."

Hobbit frowned, but said nothing. He needed the little lover, so he wouldn't say anything that might cause him to back out of the deal for that night. Maybe the task of obtaining the coat would prove to be over his head and he would let it go.

It did prove to be insuperable for the leather lover, but he got so down in the dumps, and was on his way to such a heavy dose of discouragement, that Hobbit told him he would help him get the coat. This perked up the young man from Elko, Nevada, and very shortly he was depicting a sense of western cheerfulness.

Hobbit gave Mary the woman a roll of quarters and told her to take the others down the street and have a cup of coffee. He walked in behind the building that housed the store with the coat in it. When he spotted the right building, he stopped and studied it for a while. What he really needed, he thought to himself, was a small can of contact cement. That would make a sure thing out it, and, actually, he didn't see any other way. After walking around the building to return to Canal Street, he went on down to the small restaurant where the others were. There he told them that they would have to find a place that sold contact cement and some kind of string. Before leaving, he picked up one of the plastic spoons that one of the others had used. He would need it.

They had to cross to the other side of Canal Street because there was little likelihood of their finding the right store on the side of the French Quarters.

They didn't want the big Cajun to see them, so they followed the back streets until they came upon the rear entrance of a department store. Sure enough, in the hardware department they found string and contact cement. Then they headed back up Canal Street.

Before they got to the store, Hobbit instructed each one what he and she was to do. He would go to the back of the store. California Red would stand on the side street where he could see him. Mary the woman would stand further up the street, and Little Debbie would stand on the corner at Canal Street. Screaming Girl would stand behind Little Debbie and wait on Jack Frost to walk to her when he came out of the store. He told Jack Frost to saunter up the street to the store with the jacket in it. Then he instructed them to follow his wave: when he waved to Red, Red would wave to Mary the woman, she to Little Debbie and Little Debbie to Jack Frost, who would be waiting to enter the store.

Then he took out the string and contact cement. After opening the can he used the spoon to put some of the cement on the string. He put some of the string into the can and wrapped some of it around the outside. That done, he nodded to the others to take their positions and walked to the back of the store. There he placed the can of highly flammable contact cement next to the oldest wood on the backside of the store. He needed a quick fire, and that would do it.

He then walked away from the building about twenty feet and lit the string. The fire ran quickly up the string to the can, starting the wood to burning in just a moment. He waved to California Red. At that point he left with a brisk pace, gathering up everyone but Jack Frost and Screaming Girl. He had told them that after Jack Frost got the coat out of the store they should walk straight down Canal street to St. Charles Street, then to meet him at the hot dog place on St. Charles. People weren't likely to notice a man and a woman. It's usually the different they pay attention to.

The fire trucks were rolling, wailing their piercing scream, before they reached St. Charles. They didn't look back to see if Screaming Girl and Jack Frost were moving yet. Someone might notice or, just as bad, they might think someone had seen them and it would show on their faces.

At the hot dog place on St. Charles, they all ordered foot-long hot dogs, fries and coffee. Hobbit ordered two more of each, having a positive mental attitude toward the success of the others.

Sure enough, before they got six inches off their dogs in walked Screaming Girl and Jack Frost, both grinning from ear to ear and looking like two well-dressed leather lovers. They came to the table, sat down, and dug into their hot dogs, fries and coffee.

As the restaurants, bars, and clubs opened up on Bourbon Street, people began coming in, soon filling them up. In this setting, the six travelers strolled down the street, peeking into places that had closed doors, stopping to listen to the famous Dixieland Jazz music coming out of the ones that had open doors. Most of the musicians were black, and they were good. The greatness and the ecstasy of New Orleans Dixieland Jazz lay in the live performance of the Black musicians, and there was no doubt about it, they were great.

As time wore on, Hobbit began thinking of the task before them and finally said, "It's time."

Where gaiety and light heartedness had been, a cloud of solemn contemplation came over the others. It was time, and they followed Hobbit out of the Quarter, across Canal Street on to the corner where the big Cajun drug dealer did his business.

Hobbit checked under his shirt to make sure the can of ether was still there. He could feel it, but he wanted to make sure. He had bought the ether from a guy who drove a truck for the Mission. Most of his pickups were donations for the Mission, and he said they got weird at times. Hobbit didn't think the guy was interested enough in what was going on in New Orleans, or anywhere else for that matter, to learn or suspect how the ether was used.

When they arrived within seeing distance of the Cajun, Hobbit withdrew the ether and poured some on a large piece of cotton. This he put in a zip lock bag and handed it to California Red; then he made one for himself, placing it also in a zip lock bag. As planned, the three men walked on ahead and the three women fell back far enough to keep a lookout over the scene.

The plan was for California Red to step in behind the Cajun, pop the cotton ball of ether out of the bag and put it over the Cajun's nose and mouth. Jack Frost's job was to hit him in the groin with a balled fist. Hobbit would have him in conversation about a drug deal. It was risky, even dangerous, but they would do it.

It was a piece of cake. Before Hobbit could get the drug deal going, California Red put the ether cotton over the big Cajun's mouth and nose and the drug dealer became unconscious so quickly that Hobbit almost didn't have time to grab him to keep his head from hitting the pavement. They didn't want to kill anybody, and a hard fall onto cement could kill.

The women ran up the street and helped the men carry the Cajun into the small alleyway beside the corner store. The women began deftly undressing him. They would take everything, every stitch, in order not to miss any money he had on him.

California Red stepped around the corner to take a look and spotted a red Mustang. He walked briskly back to the group and suggested that the car might belong to the Cajun. Mary the woman quickly ran her hand into the Cajun's right front pocket and brought forth a set of keys. She tossed them to Red, and he ran around the corner. When the others heard the motor of the car start, they speeded up their task and soon headed towards the sound of the running motor. California Red had stepped out of the car, his body making a slight tremble, but when Hobbit jumped into the passenger side California Red got in behind the wheel. The other four squeezed into the back seat.

"Let's just keep on going, never mind the bedrolls and packs," California Red directed the words to Hobbit.

"Keep heading for the bus station," he ordered him.

"But we've got money now, and we can easily replace those clothes and bed rolls," Red complained. He was joined by the others who were afraid and wanted to get away from the big Cajun drug dealer as fast as possible.

"Go straight to the bus station," commanded Hobbit angrily. "Do not pass go and do not go to jail."

California Red continued on to the bus station while Hobbit interrupted again, "I don't want this to ever happen again. If anyone believes he will do this again, leave as soon as we split this money. There are six bedrolls and six packs in those lockers. If we don't get them within three or four days the bus people will take them out and store them for a while longer. If that happens and the Cajun gets word of it, he just might put two and two together and come up with us. Understand?"

They did understand, and each one individually apologized. California expressed his apologies several times in many different ways to make sure everyone understood that he had not deliberately started the commotion.

"Just remember," Hobbit instructed, "I don't usually do anything without a reason. It might happen, but not hardly."

They planned to drop the car in Biloxi, Mississippi. It would be nice if they could keep it until Mobile, Alabama, but that would entail keeping the car for at least two hours and that was too long. It would be a heck of a deal to get caught driving a stolen car.

When they arrived in Biloxi, they parked in the parking lot of a large hotel. There they passed the Cajun's clothes around, looking for money. When all of the clothing items had been searched at least twice, Mary the woman counted the money. Twenty-five hundred fifty-six dollars and ninety-two cents. The best they could figure, each of them had four hundred and twenty six dollars and fifteen cents.

They divided the money down to the short rows, and had to go get some change to make it come out right. Afterwards they took the Cajun's clothes to a Salvation Army drop box, drove over to Gulf Port to get to the train yard, then dropped the car back in town. They walked to the freight yard. They were all tired, too tired to go running around all over the freight yard, so they just piled in to the first empty that had an engine up front headed east. All six soon went to sleep and woke up in the Mobile, Alabama freight yard.

They walked off the freight yard, looking for a place to get breakfast. When the lights of a small restaurant appeared in front of them they headed to it. All were in good spirits. The sleep on the train had done that.

The thought of ambiguous time caused all of them to stop and think. Mary the woman spoke up, "My heck! I've got the darn thing. I forgot it. It's a Rolex watch and there are two diamond rings."

"You hang on to them, Mary," Hobbit told her. "We'll have a hard time getting rid of something that expensive."

"Something else we forgot," chimed in Little Debbie. "The dope. He didn't have any on him, so it must have been in the car."

"I'm glad we didn't get it," Screaming Girl said. "I just hope the police search the car and find it."

"They will," California Red spoke up. "I left a note with the keys that the stuff was in the trunk. I didn't forget it. As a matter of fact, I opened the trunk. There wasn't a lot of dope, but all of it was coke, and there was just enough of it to eventually become tempting."

"We're going to have to get some grass, man," stated Jack Frost. "If we are going to have to do without a drink for a long time, we will have to have something, and grass is the only thing I can think of."

Silently, everyone agreed, but no one said anything. After eating breakfast, they went back to the freight yard to get a train going to Florida. They found an empty on one going that way, but it was occupied by two men. They invited the travelers to come aboard, so, after eyeballing the other cars and not seeing another empty, they climbed into the boxcar.

The two men were about the same size: average, about five feet, ten inches tall and slender build. Both were in good spirits and ready to answer the questions the travelers had about Florida. When the train pulled into the Tallahassee yard, the two men got off, wishing all of them luck and hoping to see them later. After a while the train pulled out again, headed east, bound for Jacksonville.

On the way they discussed the things the two men had told them, trying to figure where in Florida they would hole up for a while.

"I like Leesburg," Hobbit told them." It fits right in with my plan, and, according to the guys, there is a good Mission there. They will let you work away from the Mission, and you can take the weekend off every once in a while.

I think it's perfect."

Since they had agreed to follow Hobbit, and his leadership had so far proved to be excellent, they settled on Leesburg.

When the train arrived in Jacksonville, they called a cab and went to the bus station. When they had gotten their tickets, they put their gear in lockers; then went out to see some of the town.

Hobbit saw drug dealers selling right there at the bus station. He had heard about Jacksonville. A real mean town on the drug side. And hard to get out of if you got the heat on you. He had no intention of changing his plans for Leesburg.

There didn't seem to be anything of interest on that side of town, so they had decided to find a place to eat. Being well off with money, the thought of shoplifting for food didn't even occur to them. After walking halfway into town, they found a nice restaurant that specialized in prime rib. Each ordered that, along with baked potato, green beans, and horseraddish sauce. When they had finished, all ordered a red wine and finished off the meal with ice cream.

"That was delicious," Little Debbie exclaimed. "It was better than that other steak dinner we had."

"It shouldn't have been," California Red told them. "Prime rib and rib eye are the same piece of meat; it's just that prime rib is baked and rib eye is grilled."

"Men," exclaimed Mary the woman. "They're all so darn technical minded. They would put down a Barbie Doll because it wasn't a real woman."

Lighting up a cigarette, Screaming Girl chimed in, "Except for some things, we could do without them."

At this, everyone laughed, and the conversation turned to other possible activities to be involved in before the bus left.

Jack Frost became masculinely technical. "Why don't we get the bus tickets redated for a few days and have a good time here," he told them. "We've got enough money to get a big room in a nice hotel, and we can get a cab out to the beach."

"I've got a better idea," spoke up Hobbit. "Why don't we catch a cab to the beach and rent a place out there?"

That clinched it. They went to the bus station, got the tickets dated three days ahead, and caught a cab for Jacksonville Beach. No one thought about bringing clothes and no one had a bathing suit.

At the beach, California Red volunteered to go in and get the room. The rest of them gave him twenty dollars each, hoping that would be enough. It was. The room with bath was only a hundred dollars a night.

It was decided that one of them would buy the first jug of whiskey; the others would kick in fifteen dollars each the next day for the next day's rent.

Having learned from experience, they didn't offer to pay any in advance.

Everyone was very pleased with the room. It had two beds, and, on investigation, the couch let out to be a bed.

California Red volunteered to buy the first jug and went out to get it. When he returned, everyone but Hobbit started passing the bottle around.

Pretty soon, the talk became loud, first rowdy, then mischievous. The mischieviousness seemed more practical than the rowdy and it wasn't long before one of them mentioned going swimming in the ocean.

That opened the door to deep intellectual conceptuality. What would they use for bathing suits? The question threw ice cold water on the whole thing until Jack Frost spoke up, saying, "Why don't we go skinny dipping?"

It was a great idea. All got their shoes and socks off, headed across the street to the beach.

The hour was late and there was very little traffic on the street, but it was too dark to see if there were any people on the beach.

They took off their clothes and piled all of them into one pile—the whiskey taking effect for sure. Then all ran into the Atlantic Ocean, screaming, hollering, and popping water at each other, so you would have thought they were a bunch of teenagers.

Hobbit tired first, and, when he walked out of the water the others soon followed. Half-drunk and half-tired, they couldn't separate their individual clothes from the pile; so each of them grabbed a handful, and they started walking toward the room on the other side of the street. Halfway across the street a car came by with four boys in it. They whistled and made suggestive noises. California Red couldn't help but say something to that, so he yelled back, "Who's all that for, the women or the men?"

The boys went on without comment.

Red had to find the room key in his pants pocket, so everyone began sorting the clothes to find California Red's pants. They are tan," he told them. "Light tan."

Little Debbie found the pants and the key.

When they got inside, the five smokers sat down in the middle of the room and lit cigarettes, while Hobbit took a quick shower. Then each followed in turn, getting the salt off their bodies.

Hobbit was the first one in bed, with Mary the woman following him. Pretty soon all were in bed fast asleep.

The next morning, after dressing, they strolled down the street looking at everything in general, some commenting on the night before. Hobbit said little, but anyone could tell that he was especially pleased with his first skinny dip in his whole life, and when California Red said that what they had done was ridiculous, Hobbit philosophized, "Youth and wisdom are not compatible."

They all smiled, knowing he was almost twice as old as two of the women, and by far the oldest in the group.

When they had eaten in a restaurant that made late breakfasts, they headed for the liquor store. This time, everyone except Hobbit bought a jug, and all headed back to the room.

As soon as the others were three sheets to the wind, Hobbit went for a stroll down the beach. When he spotted over the sand dunes what looked like a clothing store, he turned off the beach to see if it was. It was.

After he purchased bathing trunks and a pair of slides for himself, he guessed at the size and bought Mary the woman a bathing suit and beach shoes. Then he headed back to the room. At the room door, he had to knock several times to get someone to let him in.

California Red opened the door with tears in his eyes. As he entered the room, Hobbit immediately saw that the women and Jack Frost were on a crying jag.

"What the heck is going on Red?" he demanded.

Sniffling, California told him, "It's that stupid dog. We left it in New Orleans!"

"Shoot!" Hobbit exclaimed. "Shoot and be tarred"

Then he put his mind to solving the problem. He wracked his brain until, finally, he came up with an idea. "Ya'll shut up a minute," he directed the order to Jack Frost and the three women, but they wouldn't obey.

"That dog," said Hobbit under his breath. "I'll kill the mutt."

He had meant it only as a psychotheraputive statement to himself, but fate would not have it that way. They had heard.

Drunkenly, all of them began screaming obscenities at him, even Jack Frost, and Little Debbie ran up to him, pounding with both fist on his chest, wailing, "You're not going to kill my little dog you mean iron-head! You're not going to kill my little puppy!"

California Red pulled her off of Hobbit, then began calming them down enough to listen to Hobbit's idea. After a little while, he succeeded.

"What I've got in mind," began Hobbit, "Is for the three men to draw straws, and the one who gets the shortest one goes back and gets the dog. If his woman wants to go with him, that's up to her. But before we draw straws, let's consider the rest of the idea. That watch and those rings can get us a lot of trouble if we don't get rid of them somewhere outside the state of Florida; so, we'll send them out with whoever goes, and he can sell them in New Orleans for whatever he can get."

That sounded like a good idea, everyone agreed. When they drew straws, Hobbit drew the shortest.

Mary the woman instantly said she would go with him. Picking up the room phone book, she found the number, then called the Jacksonville Rescue Mission, asking for the phone number of the Mission in New Orleans. With that number, she called the Mission and asked if the dog was still there. It was there, but if it wasn't claimed within a few more days it would be sent to the animal shelter. Mary the woman pleaded for five days, just to make sure she and Hobbit would have enough time. She succeeded in getting the extra days. Putting the phone back into the cradle, she said, "We had better get cleaned up and call a cab for the bus station."

When they arrived at the bus station they paid the cabbie and went first to the lockers holding their gear. With gear in hand, they went to the ticket window and asked when the next bus left to New Orleans. No luck. The next bus with that destination didn't leave until the next morning. Hobbit and Mary the woman looked at each other, reading each other's thoughts. They would hit the rails, but first they would get a refund on the two tickets to Leesburg.

The cabbie had never taken two people with packs and bedrolls to the freight yards before, and he seemed just a little bit surprised when they paid him the fare. Hobbit and Mary the woman went searching for a train with an empty boxcar headed to New Orleans. Finding one, they crawled into it and waited.

Hobbit, who now had possession of the Cajun's jewelry, put the Rolex and two diamond rings on, and admired his hands and left arm. But he commented that he'd rather have a Timex and no rings.

When the train started pulling out they discovered that they had neither food nor water, and it was a long trip to the next stop. Both decided to sleep.

They were wakened by the jar of loud banging boxcars being switched from their train to another part of the yard, but they were not moving the car they were in. When the couple stepped to the open boxcar door, they saw that dawn was just breaking, and they were in Mobile, Alabama.

"Darn" exclaimed Hobbit, "I sure didn't know I was that tired. That was a heck of a long sleep."

Mary the woman smiled and added, "Yeah. And we are going to have to get off this train to get some food and something to drink. There's no telling if it will be here when we get back."

It wasn't. They had a good breakfast, filled both of their thermos jugs from their packs with coffee, and the cook made them some extra bacon and sausage biscuits to take with them.

When they asked one of the yardmen about a train to New Orleans, he told them that the only one leaving that day was an Amtrak. They thought about it and decided. What the heck. Amtrak.

At the station office they got one-ways to New Orleans. The train had a lounge and a diner, and Hobbit had a time keeping Mary the woman out of the lounge. The diner, however, proved to be very hospitable, and the food was tasty.

When they pulled into the New Orleans train station, they began formulating their plan to get the dog. First, they would buy a dog caddy with water and food holders in it. They would get a cab and have it take them to the back of the Mission where they would put the dog in the caddy. At that point they bogged down on how to get out of New Orleans. The bus station was definitely out of the question. The Cajun had gotten a good look at Hobbit, and he would have people out looking in that area. Then they remembered the watch and the rings. That made their decision for them. They would catch the Amtrak back to Mobile.

With their plan decided upon, they called a cab and headed uptown to buy a dog caddy. Everything went smoothly, and, after picking up the dog, they had the cabbie—who had waited for them at each stop—take them back to the train station. He charged them a hundred dollars, and they asked him for a receipt, intending that the others should share in such an unexpected expense, but if not, it would be worth it, thought Hobbit. It would be worth it to keep peace in the family.

They had to ship the dog. The train people wouldn't allow it in the cars with the passengers. But the animal quarters were splendid, and a train attendant checked on Gerterka regularly.

In Mobile, they bought two Greyhound tickets to Leesburg, keeping the dog hidden with their packs and bed rolls. They just didn't want any more confusion about the puppy.

The bus didn't leave for over two hours, so they put their gear, along with the small doggie caddy, in one of the large bus station lockers, keeping the puppy, and putting it on a leash.

This time, they remembered the watch and rings, so, when they spotted a pawnshop, they went to have the items appraised.

Instead of appraising the items, the pawnbroker asked how much they wanted to borrow on them. Hobbit told him two thousand dollars. He wrote Hobbit a check, telling him he could get it cashed at the bank at the corner of the street.

Both Hobbit and Mary the woman wondered how much the items were actually worth, but, estimating by how quickly the pawnbroker had written the check for two thousand dollars, they figured they must be worth thirty or forty thousand.

After they had cashed the check, they took the dog for a stroll and food. The pup ate hungrily, devouring two large hamburgers and a large cup of water quickly. The two travelers bought burgers and cokes for themselves, then headed back to the bus station.

Boarding the bus with the dog caddy covered by their packs and bedrolls proved to be no problem. With luck, they would make it to Leesburg without incident.

They put the pup and caddy on the floor of the bus in front of their seats, then put their packs over it. The bedrolls they put topside. With the bus marked for Orlando, Florida, they believed they had it made; so they laid back and rested. They hoped the others had no trouble getting into the Mission at Leesburg, and that they wouldn't have any, either. A lot depended on Leesburg, thought Hobbit. Otherwise the plan might not work so well. It wasn't that the plan would not work at all, just not so well.

When the bus driver pulled into the parking lot of the motel in Leesburg, both travelers were ready for a rest. Not bothering to hide the dog anymore, they got off the bus as quickly as possible. The driver didn't see them because he was getting packages being shipped from the motel office. The town didn't have a bus station.

Mary the woman went into the motel office to use the phone to call California Red. He had given them the number when they had talked earlier and told them to call him and he would come and pick them up in the Mission van. When he arrived, he had brought all of the others with him. After all had hugged and kissed and shook hands, they reboarded the Mission van and California Red began filling them in on the latest news.

"We fell into it, man," he told them. "Just plain old out-house luck. Just before we got here, there had been a mass exodus. They had caught almost all of the men and women living at the Mission drinking, smoking dope and balling in an empty house on the Mission property. They were ordered to pack their stuff and get. That left them not only without a cook, they didn't have enough people to fill the work contract the Mission had with a fellow church member who owns a naked furniture manufacturing business."

They needed all of them plus Hobbit and Mary the woman, who California Red had told them were coming.

As California Red drove the van into the very large Mission property, a smile came across his face. "There is Cynthia Cook, the Executive Director of the whole Mission complex," he told them. "She is a really great person. You'll like her."

Director Cook greeted them cordially with a smile and "I'm glad to see you." She then told the two women to take Mary the woman down to the women's house and the men to show Hobbit his bed in the men's quarters. They could feed the dog and turn it loose, she told them.

Jack Frost took Hobbit to the room they would share. Being the Mission cook, California Red had a private room near the kitchen. There were two other men living in the men's part of the Mission and one additional woman living in the women's house. All of them were at work in the furniture factory.

Mary the woman was pleased with her new home. Because there were few women using the Mission, all of the ones presently there had private rooms. Hers was beautifully furnished with a mahogany bed, dresser, and chest of drawers. Two mahogany lamp tables guarded either side of the bed. The floor was carpeted with a tan shag and the two curtained-in white windows on the north side of the room allowed just enough light to come in to give it a homey atmosphere. Opening a door she thought to be a closet, she found a sink, commode and medicine chest, all very spic-and-span. The closet, she learned, was through the door near the window. After unpacking and hanging up her clothes, putting underwear and socks in the chest of drawers, she looked for a towel. Finding none, she looked for a shower and located it at the east end of the hall. In the shower room were stacks of fresh towels and other items of women's needs. She took a shower, changing into fresh clothes, and went over to the men's quarters where she had been told she would find the kitchen and dining room.

The dining room was spacious. They certainly must have a heavy walk-in crowd from the streets, she thought to herself. But she wondered where the streets were. The Mission property covered over what would be five city blocks. Its beautifully contoured terraces were partly shaded by elm and oak trees. The Mission itself was crested in the center of a jungle of tall trees and fauna of obvious tropical origins. It was enough to scare her back to the freight yards, if there was one in this town, and it sure as heck would frighten most tramps away. When she went into the kitchen, she saw Little Debbie and Screaming

Girl helping California Red prepare the evening meal. She volunteered and was happily accepted.

The folks from the furniture factory came in just before time to serve supper. They were cordial, but seemed tired and unwilling to become involved with the newcomers.

About fifteen minutes before serving time for the evening meal, a crowd began forming outside the east door of the dining room. These were the street people. Primarily, they were some of the very poor, jobless and disabled people who lived in Leesburg. They all looked hungry, much as do the street people in larger cities who eat only one meal a day. When the door was opened for them, they rushed in, grabbing the plate that was offered them, and going not to a table but to a bench that had a shelf in front of it. They did this so that when they finished their plate of food they would have room to jump up and run back to get seconds. California Red had saved enough back in the kitchen for himself and the five others. The rest of the Mission residents got theirs from the line and seated themselves at four-person tables decorated with red and white tablecloths.

Screaming Girl and Little Debbie had moved two of the regular size tables from the dining room into the back of the spacious kitchen. Put together, they were ideal for six people. Little Debbie had brought a bed sheet to use for a tablecloth.

When all of the food on the line had been taken up, California Red set the table and the six sat down to eat, Hobbit at the head of the table and Mary the woman at the other end. The other two couples sat beside each other on either side of the table.

Cynthia Cook, the Executive Director, sent her husband back to the kitchen to tell them that as soon as they had cleaned up the kitchen there would be a house meeting for them to attend. They were to be told what they could expect from the Mission and what the Mission would expect from them. All six participated in cleaning up the kitchen, and as soon as they finished they headed to the front of the building where the

Executive Director and her husband lived. Opening the door to the apartment, they entered a large classroom equipped with chalkboard, student desk, and various electronic teaching aids. Each took a seat and awaited Director Cook.

Cynthia Cook was forty years old, college educated and a very sincere Christian. She had two grown children and her first husband had been killed in a car wreck five years previously. Larry Cook had been saved while a resident of the Mission, had continued to work at the furniture factory where he was promoted to foreman, and had married Cynthia three years previously. He was also Acting Director in Cynthia's absence, especially on weekends. The title was official, but he received no salary from the Mission.

When the two entered the room, Larry sat down and Cynthia asked everyone to bow their heads while she prayed for the meeting. Having prayed, she began a talk about the Mission and its rules.

"First of all," she began, "There are a few very strictly enforced rules: no fornication, no drinking of alcoholic beverages; no smoking inside any of the Mission buildings, and all must attend a church at least once each week. This is a Christian Mission and these rules are now in effect as far as you are concerned. We also enforce the rule concerning profanity, but we give warnings before we take any serious action, because we understand that some of you have had a long history of that. The rule book contains other rules which you will be expected to learn and obey."

"Now," she continued, "About your work. Mr. Culpepper has already been assigned to the cook's job. He will need an assistant and, because you are friends, I will leave the choice of that person up to you. Mr. Culpepper will earn one hundred dollars a week. His assistant will earn seventy-five. Mr. Culpepper and his assistant will be given one day a week off from work. The rest of you will work in the furniture factory where you will begin at minimum wage. You work there eight hours a day and you will be expected to keep your own area clean, do your own laundry and, alternately, work either on Saturday or on Sunday at the Mission. You will have one day a week off from the Mission.

"You will also be expected to attend a Bible lesson in this room five nights each week. My husband or I will teach the class." Then she asked, "Are there any questions?"

All were too taken aback to have anything to say. She had been too fast for them. They simply said nothing.

Larry Cook stood up and began passing out the rulebooks. Before following his wife out of the room, he told them that they would have to give their decision about who would help Mr. Culpepper in the kitchen early in the morning.

After the Cooks left, the six travelers went outside and sat in a kind of circle on the ground, the five smokers lighting up cigarettes.

"Hobbit," Jack Frost spoke up, "How much did you say my share of that watch and ring money came to?"

"Three hundred and thirty-three dollars and thirty-three cents," replied Hobbit. Do you want yours now?"

"No," he said, "But I am sure giving this place some seconds thoughts."

The others made sounds indicating they were of like mind.

Hobbit did not allow this to separate him from the group. That would have been a mistake. Instead, he suggested that if all of them left the Mission they collectively would have enough money to rent an apartment for a month, but there would be no guarantee that they would have enough left for a second month. If that should happen, they would have to go back to the streets or the Mission; either one would be worse than it had been, and they might not be able to do what they came to Florida to do to start with.

After some additional discussion, everyone agreed to stay with the Mission for at least another month, when they would again bring the matter up for discussion.

Just as they started to break up the circle, Little Debbie exclaimed, "We haven't decided on who will help California Red in the kitchen!"

The others, including California Red, smiled at her concern and started to play a joke on her; but it had been a long day and they all quickly agreed that because she was California Red's woman she should be the one to help him in the kitchen. This pleased Little Debbie and she left the meeting happy.

The next morning at breakfast, they notified Cynthia that Little Debbie would help California Red, and also that they had cleaned up their rooms and done their laundry. This pleased the Executive Director, and she felt satisfied that she had made a correct decision in bringing all of them in on the staff. There are two kinds of "staff" in rescue missions: employed professionals, who serve as executives and counselors, and gratuity persons taken in off the streets. Sometimes one or more of the latter is put on the professional staff, depending on the expertise of the individual. The gratuity persons do almost all of the basic work of the mission, from driving mission vehicles, cooking, keeping the grounds and buildings clean and, on occasion, giving a public testimony concerning their new found faith. They are always asked to volunteer for the latter, for the benefit of groups of Christians who supported the Mission. They are never asked to lie or prevaricate; they want real, sincere testimonies.

At the furniture factory, Jack Frost signed the employee register with his real name and got a laugh from Hobbit. Percival Sullivan. It was the Percival Hobbit laughed at. He had never seen a name spelled that way before, and for Jack Frost to have it was almost unbelievable. Who would have thought anyone named Percival could be so tough and fearless as Jack Frost.

Mary the woman's name turned out to be Mary Singingtree and Screaming Girl signed hers as Jean Leatherwood. Their names had to be correct because they had to match the social security numbers they gave. The social security numbers could and probably would be checked. California Red's name had turned out to be James Culpepper. Little Debbie signed the gratuity sheet as Debbie Ogden.

California Red and Little Debbie managed to get Saturday as their day off, which coincided well with the others who were off both Saturday and Sunday. Hobbit, in the meantime, had given everyone their share of the watch and rings money, so all were fixed for cash for a time to come.

They went over to Tampa on their first Saturday off, taking the bus there and back. They had thought of asking for the van, but Hobbit said they would need it for sure later on and they needed to build up trust; so they could wait. He also told Jack Frost it would be a good time for him to score for some grass, just a twenty-dollar bag to start with.

Mostly, all they did was walk around. Jack Frost finally found a seller who handled grass. Hobbit kept a fine eye out as he attempted to make each deal. Little Debbie complained slightly that they were not seeing anything worth seeing.

When they got off the bus at the motel in Leesburg, they sat down in a near circle and Percival Sullivan alias Jack Frost rolled a joint. When he lit it, he took a couple of tokes and passed it on. It lasted one time around, but it was good weed and they were all feeling good. In better spirits than they had been all week, they walked the five blocks back to the Mission, kissed goodnight and went to their separate rooms.

The other residents were gone, checked out. They probably would not be back there for a while, if ever. That is the story of missions all over the country. People come in, get the wrinkles out of their bellies, then move on. They come from nowhere and are going nowhere. The missions try to interfere with this routine by requiring them to attend Christian services while they are there. With a few, they are successful; but they all believe that if they sow the seeds, someone down the road may reap the matured plant.

Gerterka the dog didn't know it wasn't a cat. It had eaten with cats, slept under the Mission with cats, played with cats, why shouldn't it think it was a cat? Of course, it barked instead of meowing, but it did bark in a meow kind of way. A playful little mutt, it had stolen the hearts of everyone who came into contact with it. No wonder, when it came up missing, everyone became upset about it. After they had scoured the neighborhood, calling, pleading and bemoaning their outcast states, they gave up the search and mourned for Gerterka. Mary the woman said that she believed someone had stolen it, and it was God's revenge upon them for stealing so much. They had all been stealing clothes from department stores, and, since they had a place to cook, they had lifted a few tenderloins from the chain grocery stores. This caused all of them to repent of their sins, and all of them swore off grass and booze forever. Two days later Gerterka showed up again, and everyone agreed that it was an occasion for a party, so when they went to Tampa that weekend they rented a motel room for the day and had a blowout: grass, whiskey, hamburgers and fries. When they started to leave in the wee hours of the morning, they gathered up the leftover hamburgers and fries to give to Gerterka when they got back to Leesburg.

Two months had came and gone since they came to the Mission. Several other people had came and gone. Presently, both the men's and women's houses were full.

No one in the group had mentioned the time it was taking Hobbit to arrive at a definite date when they would pull the big one. They were already in hog heaven; why fix something that ain't broke? California Red and Little Debbie were pulling down a hundred and seventy-five dollars a week. The other couples were making over three hundred dollars a week a couple. The two couples making the most money wouldn't let Red and Debbie pay for anything.

They had asked the bus driver if they could bring Gerterka with them to Tampa, but he had said no, not on the passenger part of the bus. They would have invited some of the other Mission Residents, but there was always a snitch among strangers. Sometimes, they snitched because you wouldn't do everything their way, even though you were paying for everything.

Little Debbie had her way with the sightseeing, and they had seen every water show, alligator wrestling, aquarium, zoo and nature park in Tampa and St. Petersburg. Little wonder Hobbit told them it was time for them to go to Orlando. Little Debbie and Screaming Girl screamed in delight. They had never seen Disney World. Orlando would be a milestone in their lives.

For the rest of the week, excitement sparked the air like static electricity. All six of them were having great expectations of the new weekend spot, and everything they could think of went through the telephone to a source of information. They tried again, but failed to be allowed to take Gerterka with them.

Their disappointment was overwhelming. When they got to Orlando, it took them over an hour to get to Disney World. When they finally got into Disney World they couldn't decide on what they would see first, so they just walked around and ate. After awhile, even Hobbit became tired of it and suggested that they leave. All agreed, and they returned to Leesburg early that Saturday.

The next morning at breakfast, Mary the woman said again that it was God's revenge, just like the preacher had said.

"Chasten," corrected Hobbit, then asked, "How much money do we have collectively?"

No one knew, but they all agreed to make a count and turn in the numbers to him. When this was done, he called for a meeting outside the dining room door that night.

That evening, when they had formed a near circle on the ground outside the kitchen door, Hobbit told them that they had over six thousand dollars. He wanted them to pool the money and buy a car plus insurance. California Red, who had a valid driver's license, could do the driving. When all agreed, he told them to spread the word that they were in the market for a vehicle.

They skipped Orlando the following Saturday. Instead, they used the Mission van to go around Leesburg looking at used cars. Nothing suited them. The following Saturday was the same thing, and they were almost ready to either take something they really didn't want or go to Tampa when an elderly church member came over to see California Red and tell him about a van he had in his back yard. He and his wife had been using it to go up north in the summer to see their children and grandchildren; but they had been coming down to see them during the winter. Now he felt he would save himself the wear and tear of the trip and not go up anymore. So if Red would like to see the van, he would take him out to see it. He owned a car, also.

When Red said "yes," Little Debbie said she wanted to go, too. In less than an hour, they were in the elderly man's back yard. What they saw stupefied them. Before their eyes was the most beautiful van in the world, golden tan, new tires, and not a scratch on it. But "Oh, God. How much would he want for it!"

They inspected the inside: two captain's seats, fully carpeted rear section, a small refrigerator and everything on it worked. Both Red and Debbie were actually praying under their breath that the price would be what they could afford. Finally, California Red asked the great question, "How much do you want for it?"

"Well," began the elderly man, "You sure have been doing a good job over there at the Mission, and I want to get rid of the van; but I will have to tell you that the insurance runs out on it this month and basic liability in Florida will cost you around eight hundred dollars a year for this van. But if you will take it, I will just give it to you."

California Red staggered. Little Debbie almost fainted. Getting his breath back, Red finally got out a "yes!"

The man went inside and returned with the papers already signed. He advised them also that it would cost them about three hundred dollars to transfer the title over. All Red could think of to say was "thank you," and Little Debbie repeated his gratitude.

As California Red drove the van out of the back yard into the street, he noticed that the gas tank was half full, and he decided to drive straight back to the Mission. It was almost time to start preparing the evening meal, anyway. But during the ride back, he and Debbie decided to play a joke on the rest of them, so, when they returned, they said nothing to anyone about the van.

However, unintentionally, they had parked the van near the entrance which everyone from the yard used to enter the dining room. The beauty of the van did not go unnoticed. Almost everyone commented on it, and, finally, Hobbit asked jokingly if it was for sale. He might, he said, be ready to go out and rob another drug dealer to get that van.

Red and Debbie could hold it in no longer. They began laughing at the same time, and everyone looked at them. Red told them to come back into the kitchen. There, he told them what had happened.

Hobbit had to sit down. Mary the woman turned away and crossed herself. She had been raised a Catholic on the reservation and she knew that crossing herself was the right thing to do at a time like this.

"When are we going to take it for a spin?" asked Jack Frost anxiously.

"As soon as we can get out of the kitchen," replied California Red.

Needles to say, everyone pitched in. Soon the kitchen was clean and orderly, and the six of them went out to the van. Screaming Girl remembered Gerterka and she went back to find the dog. When it came and started jumping up around her, she motioned for it to follow her and headed back to the van.

The rear of the van was carpeted completely. Only the two tinted windows in the very rear of the van did not bear the carpet layer's imprint; consequently, there was no way to see out except through the two small windows or by opening the sliding panel door on the passenger side. Jack Frost explained this to everyone and had no procrastinators when he began opening the door; but Screaming Girl told him she needed his belt, which she used to make a leash for Gerterka with which she would keep her from jumping out of the door while the van was moving.

California Red drove. Hobbit sat in the Captain's seat next to him. "Where ya'll want to go?" Hobbit asked.

"Down to see the raccoons," spoke up Little Debbie. "We haven't been down there in a long time, and there really isn't much else around here that we haven't worn out."

Years ago, a man outside Leesburg spotted a pair of raccoons foraging in his back yard. He fed the two raccoons, just as he fed the additional pair that came later, and just as he now feeds the three hundred raccoons that come into his back yard each day at sundown. Little Debbie was enthralled by the sight, as though she would never get enough of watching it.

When Gerterka saw the raccoons, a natural instinct caused the dog to lurch toward them. Luckily, Screaming Girl held the homemade leash until Jack Frost could get the sliding door shut. With that accomplished, they decided to return to the Mission for the night, but began making plans for the coming Saturday.

When they closed up the kitchen Friday night, they headed for the van. Everything, including Gerterka, was in the van: their bed rolls, packs, a small case of sterno, frying pan, olive oil, eggs, along with bread, and a beef roast California Red had cooked. They were going to Treasure Island on the Gulf side of St. Petersburg. The beach at Treasure Island has the cleanest seawater of all the world's beaches. It is also hospitable and is accessible to the public. Parking lots are available to all.

Screaming Girl had bought a leash for Gerterka, and, as soon as they opened the sliding panel door in the parking lot on Treasure Island, she removed the leash and Gerterka jumped out and ran to the sea. Undoubtedly, the dog had never seen the sea before and maybe not even the Mississippi or Lake Ponchartrain in New Orleans, and a battle between the dog and the rolling waves waged between them. Soon, Gerterka learned how to keep the mighty waves at bay by running back up the shore, and how to drive them back into the sea by attacking them and barking. This worked out well until the dog tired of it and turned to walk off: the huge wave that followed came flushing into the beach, gathering up the dog and startling it so that it like to have jumped out of its skin.

At odd intervals, all six of them went into the water, but none swam out very far. All of them had a certain fear of sharks, and, as darkness hovered over the island and made opaque the waters off the beach, that fear became exaggerated. Finally, when only the moon remained to light the sea and sand, Jack Frost called them, saying, "It's time," as he broke open a bottle of wine. Because they had money, they upgraded their drinking to a Napa Valley wine, not expensive—about twenty dollars a bottle—but good. As they passed the bottle around, Screaming Girl pulled out a lid and rolled two joints. In a few minutes, they were on their way to Stonesville.

As they sat in a near circle on the sand at the passenger side of the van with the sliding panel door open, Little Debbie posed a rhetorical problem, "Why should we anymore contemplate doing anything wrong. We have everything we need, we're having fun, so why shouldn't we start trying to do what is right?"

"I've been thinking along those same lines," Screaming Girl joined in. "There could be a lot to the things those preachers and Bible teachers say."

"Hobbit," Little Debbie began again, "You are our leader, what do you think? Is there any good in what I've been saying?"

"There's good in everything," Hobbit answered, "Even terrible wrong. But you have to remember one thing, 'Nothing is right or wrong, only thinking makes it so.'"

"Did you get that somewhere, or did you make it up yourself?" California Red asked him.

"I think I made it up myself," he answered, "But I don't really remember."

"Well, it sure is true," continued the tall redheaded man. "Twenty-five years ago it was wrong to participate in same sex sex; now everybody is doing it, even the President of the United States, so I've heard."

"You heard right, I'll bet," chimed in Jack Frost, laughing. "If that guy ain't gay there ain't a elk in Utah."

"Road kill," broke in California Red, "That's what I've been missing. Those big old elk the game warden found half dead, shot 'em and brought them down to the Helper Mission. I guess hunting season is over here now, but, if we stay again until winter I'm going to get some road kill."

Mary the woman had thought that it was not the time or the place to reveal her Christian upbringing, but she couldn't hold it back any longer. "What you are all talking about is sodomy," she told them. "And that's wrong." All of the others laughed. They laughed and laughed and laughed—grass made you do that sometimes—until finally Hobbit asked her which was wrong, to do it or to talk about it. At that, Mary the woman joined in the laughter, and they laughed a while longer.

When they waked the next morning, they splashed around in the ocean for a little while, then got the dog into the van and went back to St. Petersburg for breakfast. While they were eating, Little Debbie asked what would they do, since they had a whole day before them and really didn't have to be back to the Mission before the next morning in time to fix breakfast.

No one had an answer to the question, and they were all going through their second cup of coffee when Jack Frost exclaimed, "Holy Cow! It's that stupid Cajun!

A sensation of fear ran through all of them. They looked. It was the Cajun and he was coming into the small restaurant, looking meaner and bigger than he ever had. They got up from the table and went to the restrooms. Just as the three men got inside the rest room, the door opened and in walked the Cajun. The men quickly turned away. Jack Frost occupied the urinal while Hobbit and California Red covered the two sinks. The Cajun went on back to the full service stall and the second they heard water hitting water, they leaped out of the rest room, called the women and ran out of the restaurant. On the way out, Hobbit handed the waitress a twenty-dollar bill, more than enough to cover the cost of their breakfasts.

They saw the car. He had gotten it back! He couldn't have recognized them or he would have made a move. Or maybe he didn't make a move because he was outnumbered. The six got into their van and headed for Leesburg.

All were stunned. Their minds could think of nothing else than getting back to the safety of the Mission. When they got there, they simply sat in the van and said nothing for a long while.

After about an hour, Hobbit spoke, "I don't think he will come to Leesburg. There just isn't anything that would make him think we are here. But we have to be careful. Nobody leaves the Mission to go anywhere unless we are all together. And we need to curb our leaving the Mission. Now would be a good time for us to start learning to drive again. We can get some driving manuals and practice here on the Mission property and around the block. If the Cajun does show up over here, tell everyone immediately and we will figure out what to do. Now, how many of us don't have a felony conviction on record?"

All of them raised their hands, and he said, "I guess I'm the only one who has. So, in the meantime, we need to have a few guns. There is a pawnshop uptown that sells second-hand guns. All of you go up there and get you one, and get me a shotgun."

Town was just a few blocks away, and they arrived in front of the pawn shop minutes after they started that way. All six descended on the shop together.

At the owner's request, they filled out the forms first, Hobbit excepted. When they had filled them out, they began window-shopping. Then the pawn shop owner asked for their driver's licenses. Since only California Red had one, he asked if he could buy six guns. The owner said, "Yes," but warned that it was a serious crime for anyone with an outstanding felony conviction on his record to possess a gun, unless he had his civil rights restored. When asked what "outstanding" meant, the pawn broker explained that a person could get his civil rights restored and then buy one legally.

Hobbit made a mental note to check into the matter of getting his civil rights restored. He would first find out how it was done; then, if things went according to plan, he would hire an attorney to get the thing done.

In the meantime, California Red had purchased the guns and shells for each one, and everyone grabbed up his piece and headed to the van. Little Debbie had gotten a thirty-eight caliber derringer along with shot shells. She said that if anyone tried to hurt her she would make a hen out of him. This brought exclamations of "That'll work!" from the other five. California Red had gotten himself a ten-millimeter autoloader with cut shells. Mary the woman and Screaming Girl bought thirty-two caliber revolvers, regular shells. Jack Frost had gotten a thirty-eight police special; target shells. Hobbit had gotten number-four shot with his shotgun.

Everyone wanted to go out somewhere and practice with the guns, but fear that they would meet the Cajun drove them back to the Mission.

When the women got back to their quarters, they found a new tenant: a woman with three small children.

They immediately fell in love with the kids. Screaming Girl went down to the Publix store and bought some ice cream. Little Debbie went over to the house where the second hand donations were kept and got all three of them the prettiest clothes she could find. Mary the woman played with them while their mother took a well-needed shower.

The mother's name was Margie, the children's Alycia, Justin and Joshua. Alycia was the oldest, six, and the two boys were five and four, Joshua being the youngest.

It had been a long time since the three women had been with children in a relaxed situation when they had money to buy kids the things kids love. It was a blessed feeling for them all. They completely forgot all about the guns, the Cajun, and the big score. They had suddenly become mothers of three adorable children, and there just wasn't anything else in the world.

The real mother of the children didn't mind at all. It had been a long time since the kids had anyone to fuss over them, and she could use a break.

The six were not used to being at the Mission for the evening meal on Saturday, so they didn't really know where to sit, but the mother of the three children solved that: she left the line, took the first table she came to and went back to get meals for the kids. The other women helped, seating themselves nearby. The three men followed.

There were more men at the Mission. At first they hadn't seemed very friendly, but, when they saw the van, they loosened up and began talking to the men. You could tell that they were experienced men of the road, because they didn't speak to the women. They knew they belonged to the three men, and they left well enough alone. If they were accepted by the three men and the women spoke to them first, they would reply; but not very much unless they all got drunk together.

The three women fell so much in love with the three children that two of them, Little Debbie and Screaming Girl, approached Mary the woman and asked her if she would ask Hobbit to take the mother of the kids in as a full partner.

When Mary the woman told Hobbit of the request, he stared at her for a few seconds, then asked, "I thought you said you loved those three kids?"

"But I do, Hobbit," she answered. "And I want to help raise them."

"What are you going to do," proposed Hobbit, "If the Cajun does recognize us and comes after us with some of his men and the kids are there?"

Mary the woman thought for a moment, then said, "I guess I wasn't thinking right."

Hobbit put his arm around her and told her, "I love kids myself, and after this score is made, I just might steal me one out of an orphanage home; but right now we can't commit ourselves to any more people. It's the six of us from here on out."

When Mary the woman told the other women what Hobbit had said, they understood tearfully, and Little Debbie asked, "How much is this big score supposed to be for?"

"He told me once it could be for as much as a million dollars. He said that's why he chose Florida. This is where the big money is," explained Mary.

"Good grief!" exclaimed Screaming Girl, "That's over a hundred thousand dollars apiece. And Hobbit hasn't been wrong yet. He's put food in our belly and money in our pocket. I'm going to stick with him."

"I will too," whimpered Little Debbie.

Little Debbie was the daughter of a career service man. As a child, she moved around the world with her father and mother and, as time went on, with her sister and brother. Finally, they had settled down in Ogden, Utah, and her father had retired from the service. Without the excitement of military bases, Debbie had started drinking, but unknown to her, she was an alcoholic. Scientists believe that alcoholism is caused by alcohol in the blood catalyzing with something else to cause a "don't care" effect to take place in the mind. This, they believe, is why alcoholics have to make a serious effort to keep their drinking under control. Although some may drink reasonably for a week or two, they will soon succumb to the "don't care" effect and go on a binge.

Debbie had married a Utahan. Soon after, she became pregnant. The child was a girl.

When her daughter was eight years old, Little Debbie had gone on a drunken spree that resulted in her husband winning a divorce and custody of her daughter. Shortly afterwards, Little Debbie walked away from the world she had known into the world of hobos, alcoholics, thieves and homeless people. She had no expectations of ever returning to the life or the child she had left behind, not even with a hundred thousand dollars.

With the edict Hobbit had made concerning commitments, the women began shying away from the children. They continued to love them and bought things for them, but began discontinuing the pseudo-mother roles they had been playing. Not long afterwards, the mother received help from the Florida Department of Social Services and left the Mission. The women gave her some money and hugged the children goodbye. Little Debbie went to her room and cried.

The following Friday night, they left the Mission for their usual day of holiday, this time looking for a place to practice with their guns. As they got out into the boondocks, a truck passed them and then stopped. It was the Mission's maintenance man, who was also caretaker for the church pastor's small ranch. Both California Red and the maintenance man backed up to get along side each other, and Red asked if he knew of a place where they could shoot. He said that he did. The preacher was staying at his house in town and there was no one on the ranch other than him. He would show them a place where they could shoot. After leading them down a pasture about a half a mile where a gully provided an excellent place to shoot, he told them, "Just don't raise your sights above the gully wall."

As soon as the maintenance man left, they began loading their guns. Screaming Girl loaded first and found herself a target of a piece of a small tree embedded in the bank of the gully. She fired and hit the piece of wood with the first shot. As she continued to shoot, the others finished loading theirs and began looking for targets. When they began firing, the noise deafened them, and when Hobbit fired the shotgun they all ran out of the gully.

"That gully's too small for all of us at the same time, especially with that shotgun," Jack Frost complained for all. "Let's divide up and some can shoot while others watch."

The idea sounded good enough, and they divided into pairs according to their already-decided relationship. Hobbit fired the shotgun a couple more times, but said that the echo was too loud for him and gave it up. Mary the woman continued to take her place in the firing line.

When all had tired of firing the weapons, they picked up the shell casings, making sure they got all of them, and went back to the van. Hobbit said he would drive, using his beginners permit. He joked with California Red, "You are over twenty-one, aren't you?"

Because this was Hobbit's first time in a long time driving a vehicle on a public highway, he drove slowly and cautiously. No one complained, knowing it would be their turn soon enough, and California Red gave instructions and driving tips.

The sun was going down pretty fast at nine o'clock and by ten it was dark. Everyone began questioning and answering where they would spend the night and how long would they allow themselves to decide. It was during this debate that Jack Frost discovered that they didn't have cleaning equipment for their weapons, and they would have to wait until morning to clean them. Screaming Girl pretended to cry, wailing that she would have to sleep with an old dirty gun that night. She suggested getting a motel, but Hobbit said "no." For a while still, they would have to be careful where they parked the van, just in case someone connected with the Cajun had seen it when they almost clashed with him at the restaurant.

"How long," exclaimed Mary the woman, "Are we going to hide from that European-African-Indian dodo!" Being a tri-mix herself, she was ready to do battle with the big, mean looking Cajun, especially now that she had a gun of her own.

But no one answered her question and she didn't pursue the matter further.

Jack Frost came up with the ideal place to spend the night. "Let's go over to Alligator Alley," he said. "Maybe we will get to kill an alligator. You can kill them legally if they endanger you."

Everyone liked the idea, and California Red said that he had a good knife to field dress it with when they killed it.

When they closed up with Alligator Alley, they began looking for a place to park. Finding one, they took food from the refrigerator and made sandwiches. Little Debbie pulled out the baggie and rolled two joints. She lit them and passed them around, one to her right, the other to her left. California Red had gotten the sterno out and heated water for coffee. Everyone was soon in a complacent mood, not caring about Cajuns or alligators. After a while, they all went to sleep, waking only after sunrise Saturday morning.

Little Debbie wanted to drive and Hades wouldn't have it but that they let her. She was not really a poor driver. She just sometimes got the accelerator mixed up with the brake. She made it back to Leesburg after only running two boys and a mule off the roadside.

In town, California Red took over the vehicle driving, going first to the pawn shop to get bore brushes, cleaning rods, fluids, and cleaning pads. He also got some gun oil.

Jack Frost had gone in with him. Finding a small, portable Coleman stove, he purchased it and returned to the van. "This," he told the others, "Will upgrade our eating."

At Jack Frost's suggestion, they went to the Mission and obtained some additional pots and pans.

Hobbit was so enthused with the new stove that he told California Red to stop at Albertson's and he would go in alone. When he came out, he had a loaf of bread in a plastic bag, two small, uncooked hams, an onion and a jar of Hickory Smoke flavoring under his shirt and in his pants pockets. He handed the items to Mary the woman and told her to get some water out of the keg and start boiling the hams. She put the hams into a small pot, poured in the liquid smoke, peeled the onion and put it into the pot, put a lid on it, and lit the fire under the Coleman. California Red had been watching this in the rear view mirror and commented on the speed with which she had gotten the hams cooking. She told him that she could cook and they left it there.

They gassed up and drove all the way back to the ranch to clean their weapons, then loaded them and headed to Treasure Island. When they arrived there and parked near the beach, the ham was done.

Jack Frost went down the street to buy some wine, and Little Debbie rolled two more joints. Soon they were all eating, drinking and smoking.

"I guess we've decided to shoot the Cajun if he shows up again," said California Red.

"Shoot 'em," chimed in Little Debbie.

"Me, too," said the others.

With the scare of the Cajun out of the way, they felt free to go anywhere; so they drove up the coast almost fifty miles, then over to Leesburg.

When they got back to the Mission, there was a message for California Red for him to call his brother, collect, if necessary. He called collect.

When Red emerged from the office where the telephone was, his face told a sad story. He told them that his mother was dying and his brother wanted him to return to California right away. His brother had offered to send the money for train fare, and he would leave Monday night on the Amtrak. The others tried to console him, but he answered them with so much sadness that they decided to leave him alone, listening when he wanted to talk, but otherwise leaving him to his own thoughts.

California Red's mother had been on dialysis the past six years. She had high blood pressure, and at the time her kidneys failed her she had her first heart attack. Two heart attacks later, she lay on a bed in intensive care, jaundiced and slowly dying. She was not conscious.

His mother's death was not unreal to him. But life for him had always been life-conscious, not death-conscious. Guilt motivated his feelings of remorse, not fear. Life, that was what it was all about. Now, finally, he would lose the most important feature of his life and he felt a terrible sense of fear.

Red's father was an alcoholic, also, and had deserted the young family many years past. He never came around with love and hugs and kisses like the fathers of other children. He certainly never contributed to the support of the family. His mother had waited tables and cooked in a restaurant, sometimes fourteen hours a day, just to have enough to pay her bills and raise her family decently. The only good thing his father ever did for them was to sign over the deed for the house and land to his mother. Although there was still money owed on it, there had been a lot paid, and that helped to keep a roof over their heads all those years.

When Red spoke, he surprised all of them. "I'll take all of you out to the Highway Department first thing Monday morning. We'll just tell the people here what's going on, and Mary can take my place in the kitchen while I'm gone. She can cook pretty good. Surely one of you will pass the driving test. That way you will have a driver and be able to use the van." Then, out of deference to Hobbit, he added, "Unless someone else has something better."

Everyone, including Hobbit, thought it was a great plan and, immediately after breakfast Monday morning, they talked with Director Cook, then bailed out for the Highway Department. They had already taken the eye and written test when they had gotten their beginner permits, and they had signed the statement that they had not brought a car into Florida. The only thing left was the actual driving test. Hobbit volunteered to go first, just to show that it could be done. Jack Frost went next, followed by Screaming Girl, Mary the woman, and Little Debbie.

When Little Debbie completed her test the officer looked over his notes and went inside without saying anything to anyone. The five who smoked fired up cigarettes and commented negatively on the last actions of the officer. They had all failed the test, they all agreed. But Hobbit decided to go on inside anyway to hear the verdict with his own ears. After he had been inside a few minutes, the officer behind the desk called "Horseman," and he stepped forward. She told him to stand in the spot marked in front of the camera, and, when he had situated himself there, she took his picture. That done, Hobbit rushed out the door and told the others that he had passed.

Hearing the good news, all of them dashed inside just in time to hear "Sullivan" called. Screaming Girl screamed with joy and Little Debbie made a squeaky sound nearly a scream. Mary the woman had a big smile and a tear running down her cheek.

The outcome, amid so many screeches, squeals, and screams that Hobbit went outside out of embarrassment, was that all of them had passed the test!

As their licenses came through the computer, they were called forward to sign them and pay the fee. That done, they all headed back to the Mission, still in disbelief of the morning's event. When they arrived at the Mission, all of them rushed into the kitchen and threw together some baloney sandwiches and cream of broccoli soup for lunch. Most of the residents were at the factory, so there were few to fix for. That done, they engineered supper. From the freezer, they obtained cooked turkey, which they would thaw, chop up and cream. This would be served over toast. Cans of sweet potatoes and turnip greens provided vegetables, and they scoured the freezer for enough desserts for all. Finding enough of everything, they left it to thaw and went to the store for party supplies. Wine was out of the question for this party. Jack Daniels would have his day.

When they returned to the Mission, they left the party supplies in the van and went straight to the kitchen. The turkey had not thawed well enough, so they cut it up and put large pieces in the two microwaves which had been donated by persons unknown to them. California Red had cooked meat and vegetables and frozen them in order to have enough food if a landslide of people came to eat. He had seen that in other missions. A threat of very bad weather drove all of the people in who were sleeping out. Most people on the road preferred to sleep out, especially in Florida, where only the threat of a hurricane would drive them into a mission.

When supper was over and the six had cleaned the kitchen, they all went to the van and to the train station. California Red had packed a bag. Screaming Girl had won the straw draw and was driving. When they got to the Amtrak station, they checked the layout of the land and chose the best spot for partying and waiting on the train.

Time sped by. They had hardly gotten started when the ten o'clock Amtrak West pulled in. Red had to hurry. It would only be there a few minutes. All of the other five assisted him, Hobbit carrying his bag, Little Debbie handing his ticket to the conductor. The others made sure he didn't fall back out through the door. Amtrak serves alcoholic beverages in states where they are allowed to, so they are accustomed to having half-drunk passengers. Hopefully, Red would not drink any more until he got home.

As the Amtrak pulled out, Little Debbie felt a sudden sense of loneliness come over her. She was without a man, and this time a good one. He had promised to call. She would wait.

The next morning, after she and Mary the woman had cooked and served breakfast, one of the residents who worked in the furniture factory came into the kitchen and began making unwanted advances toward Little Debbie. He knew she was California Red's woman, but he knew Red had left and he didn't expect him to come back. Many men and women on the road would leave a mission in the middle of the night, never to be seen again. Even when Little Debbie told him that California Red was coming back, he persisted. Finally, Mary the woman hit him in the back of the head with a pot. The blow didn't knock him unconscious, but it dazed him enough to let him know that he was not in charge, and he staggered back into the dining room. Debbie asked Mary the woman to bring her gun to the kitchen. She had let California Red take hers with him so he would have a gun he could keep in his pocket, just in case he ran up on the Cajun or one of his men. Shooting men in their groins was not necessarily feminine.

Hobbit began spending a lot of time with Gerterka the dog. He cleaned her up, dusted her with flea powder, and got it a special flea collar. They had neglected to get the dog its rabies shots, and he corrected that. Soon, he and Gerterka were the best of friends and he was teaching the dog many tricks. One of the tricks they both seemed to like very much was Hobbit hiding something and Gerterka finding it. They played this trick several times each day.

Mary the woman saw this, and, although she didn't know what was going on, she thought it amounted to something.

When Little Debbie got her first phone call from California Red, she was ecstatic. Red's brother had a spare room in his home where his daughter had lived until she married, and he had allowed him to use it. He was sober as a judge. His mother was in the critical condition he had been told she was in. From jaundice and the lack of dialysis because they could not find a vein to use for that purpose, she was turning a greenish yellow. When they would give up on her, they would move her from ICU to a private room where the family could be with her.

Red could not stand the dreaded waiting. He went down to Watsonville and caught a bus to Santa Cruz. Walking down the mall in the center of the city was a familiar experience for him. There was nothing to see, actually. People came to the mall to spend money. That was that. Few people just walked around the mall to look around. He had left the derringer Little Debbie had let him have back at his brother's house. Cops here would sometimes pat down a single person to see if they were carrying anything illegal—like a gun.

When he turned to walk out to the beach, he quickened his pace. After all, it was getting dark.

In a few minutes, he was on the boardwalk at the Santa Cruz beach, looking at the pretty girls and enjoying the view of the sea. Then he spotted something Hobbit had taught him to see: a dope dealer making a sale. He watched the dealer shove the money into his pocket, then hand the buyer his dope. When he got a pocket full of bills, he would go somewhere private and put the money on himself in a safe place. They were all the same, Hobbit had taught him, with a little variation once in a while, but, basically, a dope dealer was a dope dealer.

As he walked around in the beach area, he spotted more dealers. The business must be good here, he thought to himself. There was no territory war going on. But time would tell. The more dealers on the streets here the more likely someone would make a ride-by on the competition.

He had seen enough, so he headed back to town and the bus stop.

The next day, the call came from the hospital. They were ready to move his mother into a private room. She was jaundiced so badly it would be inhumane to continue to try to keep her alive. When Red arrived at Watsonville General, his brother was already there. "How long will it be?" he asked.

"I don't know," replied his brother. "I'm keeping her on oxygen. Without it she can't breathe very well and I don't want her to die in pain."

Red bent over his mother and whispered in her ear, "I love you, mamma. I love you." Then he left the room to find an empty room with a telephone. He would call Little Debbie.

When he finished his call to Little Debbie, he went to the bathroom to smoke. Then he returned to his mother's room. She was dead. The faces of both brothers depicted the same sense of loss and shock. Finally, his brother spoke. "She was a born-again Christian, and she has gone on to heaven where all believers go. I know this is true because I am a church-going Christian myself, and life in heaven after death is the promise of God."

Red waited to see if his brother had anything else to say. He didn't. Then the doctors took the body downstairs for autopsy. His brother used the room phone to call the funeral home, which he had already made arrangements with.

Red did not want to stand for the receiving line at the funeral home, but he did. After the funeral services and burial the next day, he went back to Santa Cruz intending to get drunk.

But he didn't. He now had another woman in his life who loved him, and he was determined that he would not treat her the way he had treated his mother. Whatever the outcome, he would honor his commitment to Little Debbie.

Not really thinking a lot, his mind could not help but dwell on the many drug dealers in Santa Cruz. It had always been a tourist and college town, and that must be the explanation for the dealers. Thinking about it, he decided to play a little game. He would try to determine which dealer made the most money in any given night. The project turned out to be a good idea. It took his mind completely off the loss of his mother and he began accepting his brother's view on her contemporary dwelling.

His brother, who was administrator of the estate, told him that it would take six to eight months to get everything straightened out. The two brothers were the only heirs.

Red continued to stay with his brother. He also continued his game with the Santa Cruz drug dealers. In an odd sort of fashion, all dealers were making good money. But as time wore on he determined which dealer was the top moneyman. It was obvious. The dealer brought in almost twice as much as the other dealers. To make sure of this, Red had borrowed a pair of field glasses from his brother and watched the dealer very closely. With that done, there was nothing else to do but call Debbie and watch television. Debbie seemed to become irritated at his calling her at all hours of the day and night, so he slacked off on the phone calls. Pretty soon, he tired of the t-v.

Red thought of going over to Santa Cruz and robbing the drug dealer. "Too much light," he said to himself. "And there was nowhere to drag him. No telling who might come along to help him. But another thought came to him. He could borrow his brother's car and follow the dealer home. From that point he could pursue the matter from a different perspective. After he had gone over the idea a few more times, he decided on it. Not that he would in fact rob the drug dealer, but he would pursue the matter further.

California Red had learned well from Hobbit. He no longer allowed thoughts with emotional impetus to dictate to his mind. He weighed everything in the balance of his knowledge and experience, willing to learn more when it came along to be learned. He was actually getting into the habit of it. He didn't miss the reckless abandon he once enjoyed when he did something illegal.

Following the dealer home was no problem. Evidently, the dealer had been successful for so long he didn't suspect anything to happen. When he pulled into his driveway, Red drove on past, making a mental note of the street name and the house number.

When he took the bus to Santa Cruz the next day, California Red walked in a different direction from the beach. He circled around several streets from the dealer's house, then honed in on it. The house was a two story-brick with car—port, tennis court, and herbal flower garden. The ground floor had steel bars over the windows. Everything appeared to be locked up tight in the absence of the dealer. This latter made Red feel more confident because he did not want to have to handle more persons than the dope seller.

He went a few blocks away to a large chain grocery store to get some food for sandwiches and a fifth of low-alcohol wine. He had spotted a place where he could wait for the dealer to come home, and he wanted to be as comfortable as possible while waiting.

The wine was only three-percent alcohol; therefore, before the dealer came home, he went back to the store and got another fifth. So when the dealer did come home—around eleven-thirty—he was feeling pretty good, and just walked down to the street and started eyeballing the place.

He watched as the man opened the carport entrance to the house; then observed that an upstairs light came on, but went off a few minutes later. Then the kitchen light next to the carport came on. The man got something from the refrigerator. He disappeared somewhere inside the house, and Red did not see any lights for a long time. Finally, he walked around the house and spotted a light flickering out of a downstairs window. He crept closer, then saw it was a television set and the man was reared back in a lazy boy, watching a wrestling match.

Thinking that he had gotten enough for one night, Red walked back to the bus stop and returned to Watsonville. He had thrown away the remainder of the meat, bread and wine. A lot of people have a great misconception of an alcoholic. It was not uncommon for an alcoholic to take a drink and leave the next one alone. There just had to be a reason to back away from getting drunk. Sure, alcohol made life a little rosier, and a second, third, fourth or fortieth drink didn't look bad, except through the eyes of experience; and the eyes of experience were kept open with a reason to keep them open. In his case, it was Little Debbie. He was in love with her.

For the next two weeks, Red staked out the house every evening. The dealer did the same thing every night, except on Mondays, Tuesdays, and Wednesdays when a woman came over and spent the night with him. It was always the same woman. On other nights, he didn't see anyone enter or leave before the dealer got home.

California Red knew there would have to be an element of educated guess. He guessed that when the drug dealer first got home, he went upstairs to stash the money he had made that day; then he came downstairs to get a six-pack of beer and went into the room where the t-v was. When Red decided on this, he began working on a way of getting into the house before the man came home. His plan was to get inside the house and wait in the t-v room until the dealer relaxed in his lazy boy; then mug him with an ether rag. The same way they had gotten the Cajun.

He decided to stay away from Santa Cruz for a few days while he thought this thing out. He had a mental picture of the house and everything on the property. If it were possible to get into the house without leaving visible signs of entry for the dope dealer to see, he should be able to discover it in his mind.

But after several days he had not come up with anything. He was becoming discouraged and decided to go over and take another look at the house. He was almost ready to give the idea up when a thought came to him that would change the quality of his life. If, he thought, the dealer comes home

If he comes home and puts his money in something upstairs, it could still be there when he leaves in the morning. It was worth a try. And it was something to break up the boredom of having nothing interesting to do.

When Red got back to Watsonville, he strolled around the town, recalling things that had happened at different places. As he walked by the high school, he thought of the girl he was going to marry, the house they would build some day, and the children they would have. They even had names for the first one: John Russell if it was a boy, Bethye Lula if it was a girl. But they had never gotten that far. Jack Daniels got Red, then Jack turned into Thunderbird. Jobs ran out for him in Watsonville.

When that was finally obvious, he told his mother he was going down to Fresno to find a job, and she gave him a hundred dollars to get there and get set up. It was the first of many hundred dollars she gave him during the following four years. He kept walking, making himself tired so he would sleep well that night. In the morning, things could change.

He woke after ten o'clock the next morning. While jumping into his clothes and shoes, he began planning the day ahead.

It was noon when Red arrived in Santa Cruz, and he walked briskly to his lookout spot near the drug dealer's house. The day was Wednesday, the woman still there; but Wednesday was the day she left and it was important to pay close attention to her. He had not paid any attention before, but she could be carrying the money off with her to some other place. If that were the case, he would have to start all over again: borrow his brother's car, follow the woman home, and stake out her house. It didn't matter; he was just doing it to beat the monotony of waiting until his mother's estate was settled. But he could use a couple of thousand dollars. His thoughts drifted to the people he had left in Florida. If he got some money here, say three thousand dollars, should he tell them and share it with them? He had not resolved the question when the woman and the dope dealer came out together She wasn't holding anything. There was no indication that she had anywhere to hide anything.

As soon as they got away good, Red walked to the carport and to the door entering into the kitchen. He knew something was wrong there, but he had to find out. Sure enough, it had an electronically operated drop bar across the inside of the door. There was a key slot on the carport wall, which must be the one for the drop bar motor, but the whole wall would have to be torn open to straight wire it. He went outside and walked around the house. What he determined was that it was broad daylight; people could easily see him. The only way to get into the house was to climb a rain gutter to the second floor gable and enter a small window. The more he got into it, the more determined he was to see what was inside the house.

As he skinned his way up the rain gutter, he thought of the greasy pole contests he had entered on many July Fourth events when he was a kid. He had never won one. Not once had he ever gotten to the top of the pole to claim the envelope with the five-dollar bill in it attached to the top of the greased pole. But, he thought to himself, this darn thing ain't greased, and there's a heck of a lot more than five dollars on top of it.

Reaching the top, he pulled himself over the trough on to the roof and began sliding himself toward the window. At the window, he had to stand up, making him a target for any eye that happened to glance that way. But he worked fast. With his pocketknife he knocked a small hole in the window just outside the lock. Again with his knife he forced the lock around until he could raise the window. When he climbed in, he saw he was in a bedroom, apparently one that was being used. As he searched the closets, he realized that this was the drug dealer's bedroom.

But it was not the one where the lights had come on. He went out the door into another bedroom. This was the one where the lights came on. He searched the closets, drawers and beat on the walls. Nothing. He ripped the cover off the unused bed, then the mattress off the box springs. It was there! The box springs had been cut to allow a large metal box to sit comfortably in its center. Red grabbed the box by the handle and jerked it out of the box springs. It was heavy.

The box was not locked and he opened it by simply snapping it open. What he saw stupefied him. He had never in his life before seen so many five, ten and twenty dollar bills! As soon as he regained his mental balance, he nudged a pillow of its case and began cramming money into it. When he had emptied the box, he slung the pillowcase over his shoulder and went downstairs. He peered out the front door for a few minutes, and, seeing no one, he opened the door and walked across the street to his hiding place. When he had smoked a cigarette, he headed to the bus stop and caught the first one going in the direction of Watsonville. This caused him to have to catch three busses, but he felt safer if he was in motion

As soon as he got back to his brother's house, he went straight to the room he was using, locked the door, and dumped the pillowcase full of money on the bed. He counted the money, separating the fives, tens and twenties in different piles. There were no ones, fifties or hundreds. Later, when he had counted the money, he learned that the dealer was now fifty one thousand, five hundred and seventy dollars short.

Someday, after scientists learn to propel space ships faster, we will learn from another more advanced planet why people do such stupid things as the dope dealer had done; but for now, we must just accept the fact that it happens.

Red needed a drink, but he was afraid that he would get drunk and do something stupid, like losing the money. He did love Little Debbie, and here was enough money to make her queen of the Silver Dollar!

When his brother got in from work that afternoon, he told him that he was going back to Florida. They could send him a check for his share of the inheritance after they got everything straightened out. What Red had in mind was to send some of the money back to his brother. He would have given him some already, but his brother would never take it without an explanation of where it came from, and he couldn't do that. Later, when he didn't have to meet him face to face, he would think up a good story that would satisfy his brother's conscience.

After packing his things, he asked his brother to drive him to the Watsonville Greyhound. There, he purchased a ticket for Fresno, California. He wasn't sure what his plans would be. A kind of numbing fear pervaded his body. It was the same feeling he had gotten when he saw the Cajun in St. Petersburg, and he wanted to run from it.

His brother and his brother's wife saw him off at the bus station. It was a sad parting, his brother entreating him to stay in touch by letter the way he always had in the past.

As the bus drew out of Watsonville, he began to relax and almost went to sleep when a lightning thought jolted him awake: He had over fifty thousand dollars in a kid-size school back pack, and there were a lot of people who would rip you off just to get the pack.

When he got to Fresno, he could no longer keep himself awake. He had to get a hotel room where he would be safe and secure. The Howard Johnson would do. It was fifty dollars a night, more than he had ever paid for a room before in his entire life. His last thoughts before passing out on the soft double bed was that he was going to have to get himself together.

It was almost noon the next day when he woke. After a shower and a shave, he felt refreshed and hungry, and it was while eating his ham, eggs, and grilled potatoes that he realized that he had enough money to buy a car. It would be good to buy the car in California because his driver's license was still registered there. But no matter, he thought to himself, he would buy a car that morning. Stuffing the rest of his breakfast down and guzzling his second cup of coffee, he paid the cashier and asked her to call him a cab. When the cab arrived, he instructed the driver to go to an area with the most used car lots. The used car lot the cabbie dropped him off at covered two full acres. It was one of the biggest he had ever seen. A salesman stood in front of him when he stepped out of the cab.

After he had shown Red several of the higher priced used cars, the salesman asked him how much money he was thinking of putting into a one. Red thought for a second, then told him, "Around five thousand cash," then added, "I need something that will get me to," and panic stopped him. He had almost said Florida, and that was the last thing he wanted to do. "To Maine," he finished the sentence.

"Let's step back to the rear of the lot. I have several back there that just might be what you are looking for."

Before they reached the back row of cars, Red spotted a six-passenger station wagon that looked really good. It had new tires and the paint on it was good. Inside, it was clean as a pin. The air conditioner and the radio worked. He started bargaining with the salesman over the seven thousand dollar price tag on it. When he got him down to six five, he felt he had gone far enough, so he asked the salesman to use the restroom. In the restroom he took eight thousand dollars out of the backpack. When he stepped back into the office area, he told the salesman, "OK. Let's ride for a few minutes, and if it as good as it looks, you will have six thousand five hundred dollars in cash."

The ride turned out good and he bought the car.

California Red went to an insurance company and bought a six-month policy. He didn't change the tags, registration or title. Although he didn't know exactly what he would do with the vehicle once he got it to Florida, he knew the Hobbit would know, so he put the matter out of his mind.

With a good night's sleep behind him, he drove straight through to Tuscaloosa, Alabama before he took a motel room. Rested again the next morning, he was parked in the Mission parking lot at suppertime that evening. The other five made a big "to do" over the station wagon,

Little Debbie pointing out that now all of them could go riding and see out without having to leave a door open.

No one bothered to ask him, and he didn't tell them, where he got the money for the vehicle. They knew he was due an inheritance, and assumed he had gotten the money from that source.

The following Sunday, all of the six went to the morning church service. Little Debbie and Screaming Girl went to Sunday School.

After the noon dinner when they had finished cleaning up the kitchen and dining room, the six got in the station wagon, California Red driving, and headed for Orlando. On the way, Jack Frost brought up the subject of going to church. "I've been impressed by preachers recently. I don't know if it's them or just that I'm getting used to it."

"I like the services during the week and the Sunday School," interrupted Little Debbie.

"So do I," chimed in Screaming Girl.

"What do ya'll like most about the services?" Hobbit asked.

Well," began Little Debbie, "I like the services during the week because they are more homey. There is almost no formality, and the music is always good. The Bible lessons on Sunday morning are good, and I like the way our teacher tells the stories of the Bible. "

"They don't try to preach in Sunday School," Screaming Girl told him. "And everything Little Debbie said about the week-night services is true, too."

Hobbit was ready to let the subject drop where it was, but California Red continued the conversation. "I was raised in a Christian family, although I don't recall much of what I was taught back then. As a matter of fact, I went to church often until I finished high school. There's a lot in going to church."

"What about you, Mary," Hobbit asked her. "What do you think of all this?"

"I think there is a spirituality," she told them. "Everything is spiritual, and how we relate to that spirituality—actually relate—is the best way for us. No one way is good for everyone. Perhaps that is why the Creator made so many different ways to relate to him."

Hobbit knew he had to say something, and he spoke up, "Teach a child in the way it should go and when it is old it will not depart from it. That's a quotation from the Bible. I was raised as a Christian in a Methodist Church, and I don't doubt that when I get old I will return to it; but I'm not old yet, so don't nobody get excited about it."

Jack Frost laughed. "It appears that everyone has given a testimony, so I guess all of us qualify to get on the staff," he joked.

"You damn right we do!" exclaimed Little Debbie. "We're all on the staff, aren't we?"

"Shoot," spoke up Screaming Girl, "They just took us in because California Red could cook and they needed one. Besides, this is the old South, and they wouldn't even think about taking in a bunch of half-niggers like us." "Third-niggers," corrected Mary the woman. "I'm part Indian, too."

"Ya'll are wrong about the missions not taking in blacks," Hobbit told them. "That got over when the federal government sued Bob Jones University up in South Carolina and the local mission head was a BJU graduate. He went with BJU, accepting blacks. He fell in line when the university did. Nah," he continued, "Your race or race mix won't hold you back from getting in a mission anymore."

"Hobbit," spoke up California Red, "You sound like you're weakening some."

"How do you mean?" he questioned.

"Well, you've been telling us that we are just using the Mission until we get ready to make the big score. Now it seems you are kind of backing off."

"I'm not backing off," he told him. "Just being truthful with my brothers and sisters."

"Well, let me ask you something," Jack Frost asked him, "does that dog have anything to do with the big score? I've noticed that you have been treating it like it's the head monarch around here."

Hobbit studied the question for about a minute, then replied, "Yes, it has something to do with it."

When all the others wanted to know what part the dog would play in making the big score, Hobbit was sorry he had told them; but it's better to tell the truth to others who will soon have your life in their hands. He did, however, decline to answer any more questions about the subject.

Suddenly, Little Debbie screamed. Just as she did, the others saw in the road in front of them a huge fourteen-foot alligator. They had left the main highway and were on a two-lane road in the Florida boondocks. The alligator was just center of the road enough to block them from passing.

"Did anybody bring a gun?" California Red asked.

"I've got Debbie's derringer, but I won't get out there with it. That monster could swallow me whole."

"I've got a better idea," Jake Frost told them. "Do you have a California credit card, Red?"

When California Red replied that he did, he advised them to get the siphon hose—known as a California credit card—and draw enough gas out of the tank to pour some on the alligator. This evoked the question of what would they siphon the gas into. Nothing appeared despite the fact that they looked in every nook and cranny of the station wagon. Then Jack Frost spoke up again. "I'll use my boot," he told them. "It'll wash out with soap and water after a few days. In the meantime I can wear a pair of shoes from the donation supply."

Everyone agreed that it was a good idea, and they all vacated the station wagon, heading toward the gas feeder pipe. Jack Frost removed the gas cap; California Red began feeding the plastic oxygen hose line into the gas tank.

Little Debbie screamed again, and everyone looked in the direction she was looking. The alligator had raised itself up on all four feet, its head turned toward them. All of them dashed to the doors and jumped back into the station wagon.

"Those things can run forty miles an hour," Little Debbie exclaimed. "One of the women who stayed at the Mission told me."

The huge gator must have decided there was a meal in the direction of the station wagon, for it began walking toward it. But when it got straight in the road California Red gunned the motor, threw it in gear and raced past the snarling reptile.

After everything settled down, California Red asked Jack Frost if he still had the gas cap. "We'll have to get another one," he replied. "I still have it, but it's bent kinda double, and I think I messed in my pants, too."

Hobbit took a vote. "All in favor of going back to the Mission say so," he told them.

All were in favor.

The excitement of the alligator continued all the way back. No one of them had ever seen such a frightening thing before. Even the horror movies you could rent from the drug store and use with the VCR didn't come near the real thing.

When they got back to the Mission, Jack Frost checked his drawers. He had. And there was a strong smell of urine coming from the others. They all took baths and changed clothes. The next morning, California Red decided it was time to ask Hobbit about changing insurance and getting tags for the station wagon. When he asked him, Hobbit told him to wait until the insurance ran out, or send his brother the money to pay another six months on what he already had. But then he asked, "Why such a big deal about the wagon, anyway?"

He had not thought Hobbit would ask about it. For a second he was taken aback. Hobbit noticed the hesitation and commented on it. At that point California Red decided to tell him about the drug dealer in Santa Cruz and the money.

"You say you still have over forty thousand dollars," marveled Hobbit.

"Yes," California Red told him. "Over forty thousand dollars."

"And you still plan to stick around for the big score?" Hobbit prodded him.

"Yes," Red affirmed.

"Why?" asked Hobbit.

"I want to get off the road," Red began. "I want to take Little Debbie with me. I want the two of us to have a second chance at life. Both of us are tired of just existing."

Hobbit didn't have to ask any more questions. He knew exactly how California Red felt. Now, if Jack Frost and Screaming Girl would stick it out, he believed they would have a truly good chance of pulling the score off.

They decided that California Red should keep the car just as it was for the time being. There was no need to leave a loose end open with which someone could trace the car to Florida. If they made the big score before the tags and insurance ran out, they could junk the wagon. After all, they still had the van.

They concurred on not telling the others about the score in California or the money. Neither knew why; they just felt that way, and both of them had been surviving for several years making decisions on hunches. They did believe that something should be done about the money, so they made plans to rent a bank safe deposit box for it. They didn't have to fear the law, because the money was not reported stolen. At least they believed that. They just couldn't perceive a drug dealer calling the police and telling them he had been ripped off for that much money. The police would probably put him in jail.

Things continued to go well at the Mission. The six of them grew closer and closer together. California Red asked to be taken out of the kitchen to be allowed to work in the factory. The three women took over the food department. The three men helped clean up after the evening meal. Everyone was happy.

Hobbit had arranged for a bank safe deposit box and all of the six put their money in it. A record of each deposit into the box was made because the others didn't know about the thousands of extra dollars in the box, since Red and Hobbit had not determined when they would tell them, or even if they should—ever.

During their weekend outings in Orlando, Tampa and St. Petersburg, Mary the woman started taking long strolls around the towns alone. She had moved into the cook's room near the kitchen, thereby separating herself from the others, except during the day; so, everyone just believed she was going loner for a break in things.

Hobbit continued to play with Gerterka the dog, and Jack Frost, Little Debbie and Screaming Girl continued to go to Sunday School. Because he did most of the driving on Saturday night, California Red was usually too tired to go to Sunday School, but he did go to church. From all appearances they had settled down at the Mission, just as many homeless people throughout the United States have done.

They had been in the Mission almost a year, and Christmas was coming up again. There was no use in trying to plan the score during the Christmas season. None of them would pull it off during Christmas, so Mary the woman stopped taking her long strolls, and Hobbit gave Gerterka the dog a rest.

California Red brought up the subject of the station wagon again and Hobbit suggested that he go to another state and sell it. They agreed and Red asked Debbie to go with him. She was delighted!

They talked to the Mission Director Cynthia Cook who agreed to give them two weeks off from the Mission. When they talked with the factory manager, he told them the same thing. They both had been good and loyal workers, he told them, and they deserved some time away from Florida.

Because he had not told her about the extra money, Red withdrew four hundred dollars from Little Debbie's and his savings in the bank safety deposit box. He noted the withdrawals on their records.

They would have liked to go over to New Orleans, but memories of the Cajun kept them away from there. Instead, they decided on Charleston, South Carolina, an old historical city on the coast of the Atlantic Ocean. They had been told that the fall of the year was the best time to visit there, because the weather was very pleasant during late fall and prices were down from the summer tourist time. To give themselves some extra time, they left Friday evening after work and arrived in Savannah, Georgia, Saturday before noon. After checking into a motel and sleeping until nine o'clock that night, they drove around Savannah, looking for a place to eat, when they spotted the Smugglers' Inn. Neither had ever eaten in a five-star restaurant so they had no idea what they were getting into. They ordered the sea food plate and it was loaded with different seafood. Baked lobster tail, fried flounder and stuffed crab, broiled shrimp with scallops all adorned the plates. When they had finished their meal, they ordered a mint julep, a delicious southern drink spiked with just a bit of moonshine liquor. When they had finished their drink, Red asked for the bill. He looked at it, not believing his eyes. Seventy-five dollars! And he still owed a fifteen percent tip at the register out front.

There was no other way out. Even the Hobbit would have had to go out the front; and, besides, the waiters looked like professional bodyguards.

After they had paid and gotten over the agony of paying almost a hundred dollars for a meal, they laughed at themselves. At least, they declared, they now knew what a five-star restaurant looked like.

They arrived in Charleston Sunday morning, and they began looking for a furnished apartment that rented by the week. They didn't bother trying the newspaper because they were not familiar enough with the town.

They had driven around for almost an hour when they spotted a sign "Furnished Apartment for Rent." They talked with the resident manager; he wanted a month's rent in advance, but they told him that they only planned to stay two weeks. He compromised. A month was three hundred and fifty dollars. If they would pay two hundred dollars in advance they could have it for two weeks and the first day would not begin until Monday. They agreed, and when the manager left the apartment they sat down and counted their money. They had just over a hundred dollars left, not much for the two of them in a town like Charleston.

From the phone directory they learned that there were two newspapers that ran free personal ads. They called each of them and put messages about the station wagon on their answering machines. Red decided to ask five thousand dollars for it; that way, he could come down on the price. When they went out to get their things from the wagon, they walked down the street and got a cup of coffee and a regular daily newspaper. It was the News and Courier that they decided to run an ad in the next day. There was an entertainment section in the paper, so they kept it for later reference.

That evening when the sun was setting in the west, the two lovers drove eastward toward the beach. Soon they found it most expedient to stop at a drug store and get a map of Charleston and the surrounding area. With the aid of the map, they soon found a beach, although they had no idea which one it was. They didn't stay long. It was dinnertime and they were somewhat apprehensive about finding their way back to the apartment. They did, however, and went to one of the fried chicken places to get "go" boxes. The apartment had a t-v. It would be great to rear back and eat fried chicken while watching t-v. But before they went back to the apartment, they stopped at a grocery store and bought a six-pack of beer.

When they woke the next morning, both were still fully clothed, sprawled across two couches with chicken bones and beer cans scattered around them. They had been tired.

As soon as they had cleaned the place up, taken a shower, and done all the other necessaries, both went to the manager's apartment to see if he was going to charge them for taking phone calls for them. He had an answering machine, too, so there would be less of a chance for someone to call and not leave a message. He said he wouldn't charge, explaining that he had to charge the extra rent in order to satisfy the owners. He would tell them that he had charged the full amount, but had refunded a week of it when they checked out early. Although he had never done it before, he believed that they would go for it.

After finishing breakfast, they went to the newspaper office to place the daily ad. Then they found themselves with absolutely nothing to do. It was too chilly for them to go swimming; perhaps others enjoyed it, but they were used to warmer weather for inundating themselves in water that coho salmon would find a treat.

They had kept the paper in the wagon, so Little Debbie found a section on museums and other historical places. Both declared that they could afford that, and the first place they went to was the Charleston City Zoo. Little Debbie was thrilled by the beautiful peacocks, and California Red absolutely fell in love with the brown bears. It was so absorbing that the sun was going down on them before they knew it.

They stopped at a small restaurant and, after they had ordered, Little Debbie asked, "Red, do you love me?"

He didn't hesitate with his reply. "Yes, I do," he told her.

"Enough to marry me?" she continued.

"Yes, enough to marry you," he answered sincerely.

That night when she went to sleep in California Red's arms, Little Debbie experienced the first peaceful night of her life since she had gone out on the road years ago. Finally she felt safe from all the nightmares of the world, and dreamed of a beautiful future with the man she loved and adored.

Three days into the second week, a mechanic came to see the wagon, tried it out and offered them forty-five hundred for it. They took it, elated that they had gotten five hundred dollars more than they expected to get.

The next day at the airport they were able to get a flight to Tampa. When they arrived in Tampa, they got a cab to a motel on the Leesburg side of town and called Hobbit from there. He promised to pick them up early the next morning, probably around six o'clock. The couple made the most of the night, for they knew it would be some time before they would be able to be entirely alone again.

All four of the family came in the van the next morning. The first thing Little Debbie had to say was that she and California Red were engaged, but they had not set a date for the marriage yet. Mary the woman smiled and offered her congratulations. Screaming Girl became emotional and cried. Hobbit and Jack Frost looked as if they were thinking of how to get out of doing the same thing with their women.

California Red had told Little Debbie about the money and the drug dealer in Santa Cruz. She had left it up to him to tell the others, so he did. Mary, Jack Frost and Screaming Girl didn't know what to say, so they didn't say anything. But Hobbit, now that the news was out, spoke up. "As soon as the Christmas season is over we will begin making definite plans for the big score. Each of us will have a particular assignment. There can be no mistakes. But, in the meantime, let's all of us enjoy the season and look forward to a happy and successful new year."

All of the five applauded and Hobbit felt that he was doing his job.

The following week, the three women came up with a petition.

Since they were all going to come into some big money when they made the big score, they would like to take some of the money California Red had and buy things for poor children. They had not thought of a particular amount and felt that everyone should participate in that. Hobbit's solution to the petition was simply to ask California Red if he wanted to part with some of his money. When he agreed to, that settled the petition issue, and they decided to wait until the weekend to discuss the amount of money to be used.

When the weekend finally came, the women were all geared up for the money discussion. They had plotted, planned, and schemed all week to get at least a thousand dollars. Any more would be icing on the cake.

After the kitchen was cleaned up, the six piled into the van, heading for the beach on Treasure Island. Discussion began with positive comments about the comfort of the van against that of the station wagon. You could stretch out in the van, even if you had to leave the sliding door open in order to see out. Then, too, there would be no way anyone could trace California Red to Leesburg, Florida, through the station wagon. As this topic wore thin, Mary the woman began looking for her chance.

"We've been thinking," she began. "Little Debbie, Screaming Girl and me, that we would like to have a thousand dollars for the kids' Christmas presents."

"I don't think that would be enough," spoke up Hobbit. "Maybe three thousand would be better because we would want to give something to the homeless and abandoned children's house the Mission operates."

"I don't object to the three thousand," interrupted Jack Frost. "But those Mission kids don't need anything. I know for a fact that some of the wealthiest people in the church are buying presents for them."

"That's part of my problem with this thing," California Red told them. "I don't have any reservations of putting five thousand dollars into the fund, but how are we going to find poor kids who are not being taken care of? I know there are some in this town because there are some everywhere. But we have to spend some time to find them."

"I guess we really need to think on that," offered little Debbie.

"I agree to that," chimed in Screaming Girl.

"But it is settled," said Mary the woman, "that we will put five thousand dollars into the kids Christmas fund."

Everyone agreed and five thousand dollars became available for gifts for poor children.

Instead of spending their nights and weekends in other towns and cities, the women began walking around Leesburg. Soon, the men, reluctant to leave the women alone on the streets at night, started strolling with them. In the beginning, there didn't seem to be many kids in Leesburg who would qualify under the guidelines they had established. Leesburg is not a tourist town; it's a town wheren retired people move when they begin looking for a better place to live. It also attracts some of the winter crowd, the ones who live during the spring, summer and fall cooling it off in Yankee-land, and come down to the south when the harsh winters send them in search of a warmer climate. Of course, you have to have money to do these things, and these people have it. They also share it, especially with needy children; therefore, most of the needy children of Leesburg, Florida were well heeled at Sharing Time, commonly called Christmas.

The six were beginning to despair when California Red came up with an idea. "Why don't we just buy a motor boat for the kids in the Mission's Children's House? If we also volunteer to operate the boat for the kids, we can get a lot of fun out of it, too."

Mary the woman objected. "I don't believe we have looked half far enough yet. There are a lot of kids out in the daytime, and we have just been laying around on our behinds during the day on Saturday. Let's give this thing a little more time, and a whole lot more effort, and we'll see how it turns out. Just remember, Red," she told him, "You're part of a family now, and what you do affects us all."

"Well," apologized California Red, "I didn't mean to change anything; just came up with another idea if this one doesn't work."

On Saturday morning, two weeks before Christmas, they drove slowly past a house that had seen better days. Some children were playing in a small opening between the house and another house almost identical to it. Screaming Girl was driving with Mary the woman sitting up front beside her. She looked at Mary with a "how-about-it" and Mary nodded. When they walked up to the house, a woman in tattered clothes came out on the porch.

"Are ya'll from the welfare?" the woman asked.

With a sharp eye for people, Hobbit answered the woman. "Yes," he told her, "We are from the welfare."

"Well, I told them I couldn't do any more." the woman spoke tearfully, "and I hate giving up my kids. But they deserve a better chance at life than I can give them. Giving them up was all I could do."

Little Debbie started crying and put her arms around California Red. He looked down at her and said, "Well, I didn't really much give a toot about that boat, anyway."

The woman looked at them sort of puzzled and Hobbit spoke again. He told her they were not really from the welfare, but were concerned persons with some money who wanted to help some deserving kids have a happy Christmas.

The woman, used to people being suspicious of her, invited them to come in and look around. If there had been any doubt about her sincerity she squashed that when she told them that her neighbor was giving up one of her children, also. The woman next door only had three, but she was giving one up. She acknowledged that she had five and she was giving up three.

"How did you arrive at the numbers?" Mary the woman asked her.

"Simple," the woman began, "The church nursery over there at that Mission will take two a day and I can go back to work. Same case next door. We have to live on welfare because we have too many kids."

None of the six had actually checked on the Mission's Children's House, so they didn't know anything at all about the operation of the nursery, but all had it on their minds to find out more about it.

"We would like for you to hold off on giving up your kids, at least until after Christmas," Mary the woman said to her. "We will come over here next Saturday and take you and your neighbor shopping. Some of us will stay here with your children. And we will go now and get you some food for you and your neighbor."

The six waited until they got the van out of ear shot of the woman, then gave a great big "Huh Rah!" in unison.

As soon as they got back to the Mission, the three women jumped out of the van and ran to the kitchen. Inside, they hurried to the walk-in freezer.

There was plenty of extra meat and other frozen items there. No one would care if they gave some of it away. Besides, they did give it away in food boxes the Mission gave to people during the week.

When they had loaded up several boxes with meat and other frozen goods, they turned to the pantry where they filled two more boxes. Then they went out to get the men to help them load the boxes in the van, but they were nowhere to be seen. As they stood there in a dilemma about the men, they saw them coming from the donation supply house. All three were loaded to the gills with clothing, curtains, throw rugs, you name it, if the Mission donation center had it, they had some of it.

"Ya'll shoplift a department store?" Little Debbie ribbed them. Before answering, Jack Frost opened the rear door of the van. "Ya'll must have raided a supermarket!" he exclaimed.

"Well, don't talk so loud," Screaming Girl butted in. "The wrong ears might hear you."

"I'm going to tell Cynthia about the food in the morning," said Mary the woman.

"And I'll tell her about the clothes and things," added Hobbit.

"We sure do make a strange lot of criminals," stated California.

As soon as they threw their loads into the van, the men helped the women finish loading the food. That done, they all piled into the van and headed toward the two shotgun houses where the poor children lived.

In their haste to learn all about the kids, no one had asked the mother her name. As a matter of fact, they didn't know the kids' names, either. Screaming Girl brought this to the attention of the others and was elected to correct that matter.

They pulled the van up along side the front porch, and, to the screams of elation of the mother, they began unloading.

Her name was Sadie. Her neighbor's name was Willie. She pointed to and named the kids so fast that Screaming Girl could not remember them, so she decided to return to that later; after all, she thought to herself, they were there to help the kids, not to write a book about them.

When Sadie's refrigerator and freezer unit were filled, there was still ample food to fill another. Sadie said she could go in her neighbor's house and all of them picked up an item or more to take over there. On the second run between the houses with food Sadie noticed a box of frozen juice bars, picked them up, and gave all of the children one each. There was one left in the box, so she ate that one herself.

The other items were left on the front porch to be divided by the two mothers when the other one came home. She had been able to get a spot labor job working in a restaurant for a day, and it would be evening before she would return.

Screaming Girl wished she had seen the frozen icicles so she could have given them to the kids. She could have used them to break the ice, so to speak, and learned their names. As it was, she knew she had her work cut out for her, because these kids seemed cowed, if not spiritually broken. She had seen it before. Had it herself for a while. California Red had pulled her up from it. She knew it wasn't going to be easy.

Four of the children were playing together and she walked up to them and asked one its name. All of them shrieked and ran for Sadie. Their mother quieted them and told them that Screaming Girl was a nice lady who was going to keep the other ones from taking them away. The children didn't understand that their mothers were giving them up and believed that the social workers were to blame for everything that had gone wrong in their lives. But Sadie called all of them to her and explained that the six were going to help them. She told them that they were from the Mission and were good people.

The children began to smile and moved toward Screaming Girl and hugged her, all at one time. She lost her balance and started falling when California Red dashed over and caught her before she hit the floor. The day was saved and Screaming Girl resolved to give up the name finding and try it again on another day.

The next day at lunch, the three women walked over to Director Cook's table in the dining room, and she invited them to sit down.

They told Cynthia about the two mothers and their seven children and about the nursery situation.

"You see, ma'am," Little Debbie told her, "If they could get their kids in a certified nursery they could get jobs. But like it is, if they try something else, the welfare will take the kids. All that's happening now is the welfare is doling out a few dollars to the mothers to baby-sit their own children."

"We are aware of the problems Social Services has with poor children," Cynthia told her. "That is why we have the Children's House nursery. And it is certified. That's why we have to be very careful what we do over there. We can lose our certification just as can a commercial children's nursery, and, if that happened, we would not be able to help the families we are now helping."

Then there's nothing you can do for them," stated Little Debbie flatly.

"Well," Cynthia defended herself, "I will continue to allow you to take food over there to them. And other things, such as school clothes. I am here to help others, and I'm here to manage the way we do it in order that we can continue to do it."

Little Debbie and the two other women apologized for seeming to be overbearing. They admitted to having no experience in what they were doing and asked to be forgiven of any unintended affront. Cynthia accepted their apology.

That evening the women told the men the bad news. They were remorseful, but reconciled themselves to the fact that there was nothing they could do. When they went over to see the kids that night, they did not mention the matter.

Willie was not working that day, so she invited them over to her house. Unlike Sadie, who was medium-sized, Willie was a very big woman. Also unlike Sadie, who had a serious side, Willie exuded a jovial personality all the time. While talking about the baby-sitting problem, she laughed at the fact that she was a certified child nursery worker, but couldn't afford to put her kids in a nursery she might work for.

When the evening was over and the six were in the van headed back to the Mission, Mary the woman spoke. "Hobbit," she said, "There has to be a way we can help those people. You think on it and you will figure out something."

Hobbit replied quietly, "Thank you."

Then Jack Frost spoke up. "Doggone if I don't think we could help them if we had already made the big score. That one woman, Willie Mae, is certified as a nursery worker, so she could operate her own nursery if she had the money to open one."

"Well," interrupted California Red, "We still have almost forty thousand dollars in the bank safe deposit box, and we have our salaries, too. Why don't we open a place and hire the two mothers and let their kids stay free."

"A great idea," said Hobbit. "I vote we look into this thing tomorrow."

All agreed, and they arrived at the Mission in a very light-hearted mood, typical of the Christmas spirit.

The next day at noon, the three cooks went to Cynthia's table again, this time to quiz her on information on how to start a day nursery. Cynthia smiled and answered their questions readily. She became enthused with the idea herself, never questioning where the money would come from. After all, the six of them together were averaging over six hundred dollars a week from the factory, plus another two hundred in the Mission kitchen. They could easily make payments on a nursery as well as pay minimum wage salaries.

Needless to say, the next day was a confusion of running quickly to see the two mothers, finding them in different places at different times, requiring several trips in order to explain the idea and get their approval for it. They gave their approval, although they indicated that they didn't really understand it. Much more time of the day was consumed working in the kitchen and the furniture factory. Excluding eating, smoking, and going to the bathroom, the remainder of the day went to phone calls to real estate agencies.

There were many real estate agencies for Leesburg and the surrounding area. Some even had listings for Tampa and Orlando. Finally, it was decided that one of the women would make phone calls and the men would help with the kitchen and dining room each meal they were there. This worked out much better, and they soon had evening and weekend appointments with real estate agents to look at buildings with yard space.

Christmas was a winner! All of the six gave presents to each other. They donated two thousand dollars for presents to the eight children and their mothers, plus additional money for food and rent. Red had a phone put in Sadie's house. Of course, Cynthia Cook received a gift of perfume and powder. Most of the residents were gone for the holidays, due mostly to the fact that they were working in the factory and were loaded up with cash. But a few, especially the ones who helped with the Mission, stayed. The six bought presents for them, too. For the very poor and homeless who came Christmas Day, the Mission and the six gave a special bag of goodies. The Mission bag consisted of apples, oranges, tangerines, a pair of socks, a toothbrush, and toothpaste. The bag the six gave them contained two packs of cigarettes, two mini bottles of Jack Daniels, a box of matches and a card with two dollars in cash in it. There were many smiles on the faces of the poor and homeless people as the left the rear of the Mission's yard. Cynthia Cook noticed this and was very pleased.

The six had hoped to have found a house by the new year; but that was not to be. Mostly, the ones they saw were too small. They had hoped to get one that would be big enough to house the two families and contain the day center, but, after January came and went, they thought they would have to give up on that idea.

They, in the meantime, were paying the rent and utilities on both houses.

As Valentine's Day approached, the six were despairing of the idea. They just didn't have enough money. The families couldn't survive on two minimum-wage salaries and pay rent, utilities, and buy other necessities. Giving them a free place to live was the only way to make the idea possible.

Wednesday before Valentine's Day, a real estate agent, who had already shown them three houses, called. The surprise gave way to expectation. The agent, a woman named Betty Cauldwell, knew why they were looking for a large house.

That evening, Betty Cauldwell came to the Mission and led them to the house. It was an old southern plantation-type house, still in good repair, and it had a current valid inspection sticker on it. There were nine rooms and two-and-a-half baths. There was also a shotgun house in the rear which was still usable.

Little Debbie was the first to ask, "How much is it?"

"It won't cost you anything. The person who is getting rid of it is paying me to find a taker, and all he wants is a receipt that he can use to deduct the place from his taxes." Then she added, "His lawyer has drawn up a paper he wants you and the agent from social services to sign. It states that the gift of this building and property will get two families off of welfare, and will be used as a business location for six other homeless people."

"My God!" exclaimed Hobbit, "We can get the Mission and the Salvation Army to donate beds, stoves, washers, dryers, and refrigerators. We can buy them a home freezer, and the things necessary to operate the nursery. I'm ready for it, myself."

The others quickly concurred. Screaming Girl said it seemed like a blessing from God.

The next two weeks were filled with hard and sometimes exasperating work. The place had to be sanitized; furniture had to be moved in; appliances put in place. The floors of the house were of beautiful hardwood, so they decided not to carpet or put down rugs. Instead, they hired a floor finisher, and he turned them into something wonderful.

Another blessing came in the person of the social services worker. She obtained the use permit for the house and the business license for the nursery.

By the first week of March, the house was ready to be moved into, and everyone involved agreed to have a special party that Saturday. The six agreed that there would be no whiskey, and all cigarette smoking would be done outside. The real estate agent, Betty Cauldwell, would be there to hand over the deed to the house. Although most of the money spent on the house had come from California Red's cash, everyone, including California Red, voted that the deed should be in Hobbit's name. Hobbit had won not only their respect and admiration, but also their love. To the six, there was no greater leader in the whole world. Without him, they would still be in Utah or some other western state eking out an existence, and drowning their dreams in Thunderbird wine. Now each of them felt like they were somebody, the most precious thing any human being has. Their gratitude grew each time the line of homeless people came into the Mission dining room to have a meal. They thanked the Lord for Brooke Eugene Horseman, alias Hobbit.

He had led them to success in every way and the deed was their way of saying "thank you".

The two mothers and three women had made a great effort on the downstairs of the house. It was sensuously young. The mother of every child left there would feel that she was leaving her presence in the building.

Outside, the men had erected swings, slides, miniature tree houses, bocce ball runways, and a small softball field. There had been a debate about a dog and a cat, but no decision had been made. A little later, perhaps.

Cynthia Cook and her husband Charles had been invited, along with several people from the church. The social services representative planned to bring four of her co-workers. Betty Cauldwell had agreed to ask the person who donated the place to come, and there would be several relatives of the two mothers. California Red had spent much of the day in the Mission kitchen preparing hors d'oeuvres, much to the delight of those who recognized his great talent for cookery. Dress was to be informal.

Willie Mae appointed herself as official greeter and did a great job of it. Everyone entering the house felt a warmness within themselves for being present. Betty Cauldwell passed the word along that the previous owner could not come.

When the food was almost gone, Hobbit told Mary the woman that he was ready to make his speech. She told the others of the six, and they began tapping their paper cups with their plastic spoons, shouting "Quiet, everybody!" When everyone had gotten quiet, the three women and two men looked in the direction where Hobbit was standing. Others in the crowd followed suit, and soon they were all looking at Hobbit. He was glad he had not had a drink. At least any mistakes he should make would be attributed to his ineptitude at speechmaking.

"Folks," he began, "I can't really tell you how great an experience this is for me tonight, and I know for sure that I speak for the two mothers, the children, and the six of us who had the idea. You have created a milestone in our lives, and the many children who will enjoy the use of this nursery should know who their benefactors are. So, to you who helped with the things necessary to establish this nursery, and to the owner who donated it to us, we want to give you our sincere thanks." At that point a loud round of applause broke out and lasted for almost a full minute. "But we want to do more than tell you how much we appreciate your help. We want to pass the word along to everyone who comes into this house; so we have made a brass plaque with each of your names emblazoned on it, which we will place in your honor just inside the front door."

Another round of applause, and Hobbit waved his right hand, saying "Thank you. Thank you." He was joined by others of the six as well as the mothers, their relatives, and some of the children.

They had not done anything about the shotgun house at the far rear of the property. It was so-so on needing a paint job; the inside would pass if the kitchen and bathroom were cleaned. Hobbit asked California Red if he could afford any more money toward the project. Red anxiously agreed to finance the restoration of the shotgun house.

On Wednesday of the following week, their ad came out in the morning newspaper. By afternoon, Sadie called Hobbit to ask him if he could get them a cordless telephone, because they were going crazy running from one place to another to answer the phone. People were calling from everywhere to make appointments to come and see the new nursery. Hobbit said he would bring one when they came over that evening. He also told her they were bringing materials with which to restore the shotgun house.

A shotgun house is so called because one might fire a shotgun into the front door and the blast would go out the back door. It had a living room, a dining room and kitchen on one side, and a bathroom in between the two bedrooms on the other. In some places in the southeastern United States, a shotgun house will accommodate as many as eight adults. According to the number of adults using the house, the number of children would arithmatically increase. Two families, for example, might have a total of ten kids, making the occupancy fourteen.

While the two mothers showed the prospective clients the house and play areas, Hobbit and the others cleaned the bathroom and kitchen of the shotgun house. They had put a fence around the entire property with only one gate for entrance and it was in front where the guests were parked. They preferred not to ask them to move their cars; so they continued to clean the house, occasionally stopping to discuss what they would do with each room.

"What are we going to do with this house?" Little Debbie asked Hobbit.

"Well," he answered, "We're going to put a fence up that will make a square around the house. Then we will put up a high wooden fence inside the wire fence. But before we do all that, we will cut us a hole in the back fence and put us a gate and lock on it."

"Which means," interrupted Jack Frost, "We will have to turn one of these rooms into a bedroom."

"Exactly," Hobbit stated. "And the dining room will be our party room. We can create a lot of privacy there."

Screaming Girl spoke up. "But when are we going to do the big score? We have been here over a year and all we've got is a shotgun house and ownership of a very small business. I was hoping for more than this."

"It'll come," promised Hobbit. "As soon as we get this house together we will start making definite plans to make it." He could have added that Mary the woman had the deciding information, but he felt that she might weaken under questioning from the other two women and tell them what the plans were, and he didn't want to do that until go-time.

When the house was restored, it was a wonder of modern technology. It had aluminum siding, a new green roof; the chimney had been restored and a windmill stood guardian over its top. Air conditioning and a heat pump had been installed. Because the floors were hardwood, they had not put carpet down. The walls were papered; a new commode and kitchen sink had been put in, along with a new stove and refrigerator, and the back stoop had been closed in to accommodate a washer and dryer. Each couple had purchased their own bedroom furniture.

The nursery was doing exceptionally well. The two mothers had forty children at ten dollars a day, for a total of two thousand dollars a week. They had given Sadie and Willie Mae a raise to two hundred and twenty-five dollars a week. Their expenses, including insurance and utilities, ran to a total of twelve hundred and fifty dollars a week, leaving then with a profit of seven hundred and fifty dollars a week. Multiplied by fifty-two, this gave them an income of thirty-nine thousand dollars a year.

Hobbit told them that, with all done, they would party that weekend.

When they awakened that Saturday afternoon after an all-night party in their new house, everyone needed a drink and a cup of coffee. All but

Hobbit needed a cigarette. One-and two-at-a-time, they trickled into the party room, none having much to say. A "Good morning" was considered sufficient to show that empathy still existed. They had not been rowdy, but had put away a lot of alcohol and marijuana. As the last one came in, Hobbit spoke. "Next Saturday is go-time," he told them. "We will drive over to Tampa Friday night, then back to the house. About noon Saturday we will return to Tampa, have lunch, and go to work. You will be told what is happening just before we start to work."

The winds of discontent began blowing Tuesday evening when Sadie and Willie Mae told them that they would have to have more help. They said they just couldn't take care of forty kids. Both of them were running themselves ragged, and the kids were not being properly cared for. They said two additional workers were needed.

Hobbit got the request from Mary the woman third-handed. Little Debbie was the original receiver of the information, so he did the most logical thing he could think of: he called Little Debbie to join with him and Mary the woman to arrive at a decision on the matter. They settled on two additional helpers at five dollars an hour. When the information was conveyed to Sadie, she promised to find two suitable persons for the jobs.

Finding two people suitable for work in a child care center at five dollars an hour proved to be a tough job, and, when all else failed, the two mothers approached their church Pastor about the matter. They explained that the center was for people who couldn't afford to pay more than ten dollars a day. The jobs were sort of a ministry, they told him.

The Pastor recognized their plight, and, the following Sunday morning, he spoke for a few minutes from the pulpit concerning the spiritual value of giving of one's self. Then, after describing the nursery operated by Sadie and Willie Mae, he asked that two available persons take the jobs for the salary of five dollars an hour. As the Lord would have it, two retired ladies volunteered to accept the jobs, both had experience in child-care work.

Friday was on top of them before they knew it. Screaming Girl and Little Debbie had announced they were going to attend the Bible lesson that evening, no matter what. Both believed the Lord was leading all of them to make the big score Hobbit had lined up, and they planned to stay on His good side. Each realized that her life could be at stake during and after the venture. Both were ready to go all the way as long as they believed God was on their side. There was no neutral ground: God was either for you or against you.

After supper the six cleaned up the kitchen together, and Hobbit told them that all of them might as well go to the Bible lesson because they would have to wait on Screaming Girl and Little Debbie.

All attended the Bible lesson, and, after it was over, they went to the little house on the nursery property. Jack Frost made a pot of coffee while the others did various things and another. Soon, everyone settled down in the party room and Jack Frost played "Papa" and served the coffee.

Hobbit spoke. "Mary the woman will be leading the way tonight. She has all of the targets identified, and we will hit as many tonight as we possibly can. Safely, of course." Then he pulled a bottle and a can from his pockets. "These," he told them, "Will be our weapons tonight." Picking up the bottle, he explained, "This is a hot sauce Mary the woman made from the hottest South American and Chinese peppers. One drop of it on the tip of your finger will cause your skin to burn any where the finger tip touches; and, in some parts of the body, the pain of the burn is intolerable: no one can stand it." Picking up the can, he continued, "This is the best sunburn pain killer there is. It will stop the pain of any surface skin burn. Together, these two things will make anyone tell us what we want to know; and what we want to know is: the names, addresses, and descriptions of the persons they are buying their drugs from. We will be hitting the street dealers Mary the woman has been lining up during the past few months, and we will be looking for drug Kingpins."

"You know something, Hobbit," Screaming Girl spoke up, "If you had not been so successful so far, I'd believe you're crazy as a Scottish loon"

"So would I," agreed Little Debbie. Jack Frost just sat and shook his head. To him it was the darndest thing any fool could come up with, but he knew Hobbit was no fool. "I'm still in," he announced.

"I'm still in, too," exclaimed Little Debbie.

Screaming Girl followed suit; California Red and Mary the woman felt they didn't have to say anything. They were in.

Hobbit declared that he would drive and Mary the woman would ride shotgun. Mary, he explained, would have to be where she could direct him to the targets. He would visually survey the area and assign each person a specific task according to the need. They would use ether as they had done in New Orleans, and he had bought four sets of handcuffs to restrain the dealer when he awoke. Stocking caps were available for use for blindfolds. They would not use guns. It was their belief that they were not breaking the law stealing from illegal drug dealers, and that would remain true as long as they didn't kill anyone.

Mary directed Hobbit to drive to St. Petersburg. When they got in town, she told him to head north. Soon, Hobbit could see street dealers on every corner; but Mary said nothing. When the street dealers disappeared, she told him to slow down.

Another block and he saw him. "I believe you're right, Mary," he told her. "He has protected territory. That means he is part of a gang. And it means big money, too."

The side door to the van was closed, and Hobbit had to instruct the others in detail.

"Jack," he began. "This isn't a big guy, so you use the ether. Remember, you have to hold the ether rag over his nose and mouth until he starts sagging."

"Red," he continued, "You help Jack put him into the van. I will drive up right beside you as soon as I see him sag.

"Debbie, you and Screaming Girl get out those hand cuffs and a cap to pull over his eyes. It's important that he doesn't see us. One of you cuff his legs together, the other get the wrists."

He let California Red out at the far corner on the same block the street dealer used. Jack Frost he let out on the corner above the dealer. There he stopped the van, and Mary the woman took up her position where she could peek around the corner. At that point, all systems were go.

When Jack Frost got directly in front of the street dealer, he pointed to California Red coming from the other corner, and asked flatly, "Who's that?"

When the dealer turned his head and fixed it for just a few seconds, Jack Frost mugged him with the ether rag. He had to hold on to him with everything he had. The street dealer was tough and agile. As long as he was conscious, he knew what was going on, and he fought it all the way. As soon as he saw the dealer wasn't going to go down, California Red broke into a run and the long-legged Californian was by Jack Frost's side in seconds. Then, with the two of them on the job, they brought the dealer down sound asleep. Mary the woman had motioned Hobbit forward with the van, entering it herself as it turned the corner, and they were at the site of the action immediately.

Mary jumped out and pushed the side door of the van back, and, when Jack Frost and California Red threw the dealer into it, Little Debbie and Screaming Girl cuffed him and pulled the stocking cap over his eyes.

When all were back in the van, Mary the woman pushed the side door closed. She got in, instructing Hobbit to go straight to the other side of town. There, an abandoned house awaited the six and their dope dealer. There he would talk.

As they carried him inside, the dealer began regaining consciousness. Hobbit told them to hold off on the ether so they could start questioning him right away. They handcuffed him in a utility room to what must have been a sewage pipe. Then they began asking him to tell them the name, address, and description of the person who he bought his dope from. When he wouldn't tell them, the three girls pulled his pants and shorts down to his knees and put the hot sauce on his penis and testicles. In a minute, after being told that they could stop the burning, he, through screams, agreed to talk. The girls sprayed him with the pain reliever.

Hobbit, Jack Frost and California Red had a round with the street dealer. When they thought they were getting pretty much the same story from him, they asked the women to take over and make a determination. When all of them had grilled him thoroughly, they compared stories and believed the dealer had been telling the truth.

Hobbit told them to put him back to sleep and carry him to the van. He made sure they had not left anything that would identify them; then went to the driver's seat. He drove down to the beach on Tampa Bay while telling the others to search the dealer for any money and valuables. He vetoed strip searching him because of the thing with the Cajun and the fact that he had been in St. Pete earlier. He didn't want a method of operation identifying them.

He had a watch, ring, gold necklace, and four thousand dollars. Being the weekend, that was about par for the street. The protected territory was not doing him any good.

After dumping the dealer on the beach, they took the handcuffs off of him. Jack Frost was still a little shaken because the dealer almost got away from him, so they decided to return home for the night. They stopped by the grocery store, got some wine and canned soup, then headed to the shotgun house.

The next Saturday night in Orlando was pretty much the same. Mary the woman had picked the easiest target and had located a house in which to interrogate him.

The money improved. They got over six thousand dollars, plus jewelry.

Sunday being a holy day, they decided to save up on them so they could use one on a Kingpin, if necessary. They made it to services in the sanctuary, but missed Sunday School.

After church, they went out to eat, then back to the shotgun house to divide the money they had taken in Friday and Saturday nights. When they gave it a more exact count, it came to ten thousand, eight hundred and thirty-five dollars. They took eighteen hundred dollars each and put the remainder in the kitty jar.

Tuesday morning, while five of the six were at their special table in the kitchen eating breakfast, Mary the woman came in, a frightened look on her face, telling the others that the newspaper she held in her hand contained bad news for them. Without saying any more, she tossed the morning paper into the middle of the table. The headlines told the whole story, "SUSPECTED DRUG DEALERS SHOT." The news story went on to say that suspected drug dealers in St. Petersburg and Tampa had been shot in a drive-by. There was also a suspicion of a drug gang war.

When Hobbit had read the rest of the story, he laid the paper down and spoke to the others. "It appears that we have started a drug war. The best I can make of it is that the two dealers we hit belonged to two different factions, and each thinks the other did the hit we made. They must believe the other is lying when he says he got hit, too."

Little Debbie had an expression of concerned sadness on her face. "I thought we would not kill anyone," she said with a grimace.

"The paper doesn't say they were killed," spoke up Mary the woman. "Maybe they will live."

"What we need to do right now is decide if we are going to continue with this thing. If we do continue, we must hit the Kingpins right away. If we wait, they will have so much security around themselves we won't have a chance to hit them."

"I vote that we think about it today, and go over to the house tonight to discuss it and make a decision," California Red suggested.

The others thought it was a better idea and the matter was reprieved until after supper that night.

At the shotgun house, no one seemed to want to be the first one to open the subject. The possibility of death had become more imminent and the score did not seem so lucrative anymore. There was little need of getting off the road if you were going to be hunted down and killed. Better a live hobo drunk than a dead rich man.

Finally, Jack Frost broke the ice, "I have thought of nothing else all day but the position we are now in about the big score. With all the thinking I could do, I never managed to come up with anything positive or negative; the two are too well balanced out. So I think this: the whole thing is a gamble to start with. There never has been anything certain about any of it. Why not let a gamble decide for us? We'll pick two of us, one for it and another against. They can toss coins to the line and the best four out of seven wins."

"Where in the heck did you all of a sudden get all them brains from?" Screaming Girl asked, laughing.

"Darn right," chimed in Little Debbie. "You ought to be a preacher."

"Let's vote," California Red decided. "All in favor of Hobbit tossing for the do-it side say aye."

Hobbit was elected for the do-it side, but no one could be decided upon to toss for the don't-do-it side. After quite a bit of hassle they hit upon the idea of odd man out and began shaking coins. When the final choice lay between Mary the woman and Jack Frost, there was a lot of tension in the party room of the shotgun house. Both Jack and Mary were good at coin tossing, but Mary was Hobbit's woman and, if she lost the final toss with Hobbit, the others would feel uncomfortable with the outcome.

Jack Frost won the odd man, and would toss don't against Hobbit's do. The four others argued over the line they should toss to, but finally ruled on a long thin crack in the floor between the party room and the kitchen.

Hobbit was leading Jack Frost three to two at the beginning of the sixth toss when Jack's coin hit, bounced, turned on its side and rolled. It went into the kitchen, over three feet from the line. Hobbit effected a flat toss and landed several inches from the line.

"Well," spoke up Screaming Girl, "That means Hobbit is still in charge. So who do we kill next?"

"That's not fair, Screaming Girl," Hobbit complained. "We will plan out everything really well in order to do all we can to avoid killing anyone ourselves; but I can't be responsible for what other people do."

"I'm sorry, Hobbie," Screaming Girl apologized. "I didn't mean it that way."

"Darn it," he shouted, "My name is Hobbit. I'm no darn sissy."

Screaming Girl decided to not pursue the matter any further.

"Well, Hobbit, what's our next move?" asked California Red.

"We might have to move out of the Mission," he answered. "There is little time to do the work we need to do. We need to watch those Kingpins' houses, and that's something you do well, Red, since you've already made one good score watching. So why don't you tell Cynthia tomorrow that you are moving out."

California Red agreed, and the next morning after talking with the Executive Director he packed his things into the van and moved to the shotgun house. When he had finished that, he drove over to the Gulf side of Florida to find the two Kingpins' residences.

Neither residence was as impressive as he had imagined. Even taking into account the price of real estate on the Gulf side of Florida, the houses and the property around them just didn't seem pricey enough for a Kingpin drug dealer. This, he knew, would take a lot of watching.

When he returned to the Mission to get the others, he told them about his concern and suggested that Mary the woman be staked out at one of the houses until she could establish the identity of some of the street dealers she had seen on her walks through the cities. As much as he did not want to believe it, they could be on a bum steer.

Mary the woman agreed. She left the Mission and moved into the shotgun house, taking the room she and Hobbit shared.

California Red dropped Mary the woman off near one of the houses. She found her own spot and sat in for a long watch. Red parked about a half of a mile away and watched her through binoculars. When the afternoon was over, he drove up near her spot and she walked briskly to the van.

"This is one of them," she told him. "I saw three street dealers go inside. They didn't stay long. About long enough for the man to count his money and give them their dope."

"OK," he told her. "Tomorrow I will take you down to the other house."

When they left the Mission that night, Hobbit brought Gerterka the dog with him. He also had a wooden box about two feet square and four inches high which he said he would make a house box for the dog to use inside. His purpose, he said, for bringing the dog now was to house train it. It was a very important dog, he told them.

An hour of very quiet whispers passed among the five alcoholics until, finally, California Red appointed himself to speak to Hobbit. "Hobbit," he began, "We want to know if you are planning to steal these dealer's drugs and, if so, what are you planning to do with them?"

Hobbit had anticipated the question being asked sometime, and their asking it right on top of his bringing the dog pleased him. They were fast thinkers, all of them, and they would pull off these scores with ease.

"That's not what the dog is for," he told them. "But if we stumble upon their dope, we will pour it into their bathtubs and run water over it until it goes down the drain. I'm not even thinking about getting into the drug business."

Relieved, the alcoholics smiled and gave him a round of applause. If you ever want to get someone who is against, get a former. That applies to everything. With alcoholics, when they determine to quit or control their drinking, they turn against other forms of recreational drugs, also. They continued to drink every once in a while, but their group, especially with Hobbit, who was not an alcoholic, was strong enough to control it and not let it control them.

When they got to the shotgun house and fixed Gerterka's litter box, Mary the woman told them about the events of the day. She told them that she had not been able to determine how many people were resident in the house, but, judging by the size of it, there would be no more than two bedrooms. Both she and California Red stated their reservations about them being Kingpin houses.

"These people might be in-betweens," Hobbit speculated. "In the old days, the language ran from pusher, who we now call a street dealer, to dealer, and then to Kingpin. These outfits might be set up along those lines, and, if that's true, we have another step to go to get to the top where the real money is."

"I'm for going all the way," Jack Frost spoke up, and the others followed in chorus, "We're going all the way."

Because of the gang war threat, they decided to just drive over to Orlando and observe what was going on. They found it was business as usual. There were no stake-out security persons there to protect the street dealers. Since they now believed it was a chance of good fortune or the will of God that they had hit two rival gang dealers, they decided not to chance another hit on a street dealer, because it might tip them off that it wasn't a rival gang who hit the ones that were fighting the war. When they had done with their prowling for the evening, they went back to the Mission where the four got off. Mary the woman and California Red returned to the shotgun house.

Gerterka had already learned to use her litter box, and Mary sifted out the lumps with a colander spoon, throwing them out into the back yard. After she had thrown them out, she thought better of it and planned to remind herself not to do it again. A safe place over in the corner of the yard would keep people's feet cleaner.

Red and Mary had not worked as they usually did during the day and they were not tired, so Red suggested they have a drink of the champagne in the refrigerator, then start cleaning up the house. Because they had not drunk for a while, the alcohol hit hard, and both of them soon stumbled to their rooms and went sound to sleep.

When morning came and both had showered and drunk a fourth cup of coffee, they got into the van and proceeded to the other Kingpin's house. When Mary had picked out a good spot, she told Red to stop and she got out. She told him that she would be hungry and in need of more coffee by noon, and he would have to leave the area and get the stuff. He complained that he didn't like the idea of leaving her there alone, but she insisted, adding that if they spotted her they would kill her anyway.

Nothing happened. The day went well. When Mary returned to the van, she said that this was the other house. She had seen several drug dealers she knew and some she didn't know enter the house.

When they reported the day's findings to Hobbit, he told them that they would have to watch the houses in the evening in order to determine when the least number of people would be there. Everyone could participate; they should be able to do both houses at the same time, and they would start that night. "We are going to have to make another major decision as we determine when and how we can hit these houses, and we had better start thinking about it now. The question is, if we determine that these are middlemen, do we hit both Kingpins the same night, or wait? If we don't wait, it will mean hitting them cold, and hitting them cold means we have to use guns. If we wait, they will be ready for us and we will have to carry our guns." Hobbit left it there. He saw the expressions on their faces when he mentioned using the guns and he knew not to go any further.

There was little activity at either house that evening and all agreed that they would have to make all-night surveillance of both houses in order to determine when and how they should hit them.

Hobbit advised them that all of them would have to move out of the Mission and into the shotgun house.

"We are going to have to make another decision to determine how we will hit these houses. If we get the information on the major Kingpins, we can begin planning on that right away. I don't like the idea of walking into an ambush."

Jack Frost was the first one to speak up. "I think the idea of three hitting each house is good enough, if we determine that three can do a house. If not, we had better all stick together, and if we have time to do both houses tonight, ok; but if we don't, we'll do the other one later. Just remember, we will have to interrogate the ones there to find out about the major Kingpins."

"I say play it by ear," California Red told them. "We will use the information we have along with what we see when we get there. That sounds a heck of a lot safer than going in on some rigid plan that might fall apart at the start."

"And these people will have guns," added Little Debbie.

Debbie's statement about guns evoked a response from Screaming Girl. "I think we should all do one house at a time," she told them. "Four go in and two hang back, watching from the outside to see if we need guns. I know that no one of us wants to kill anyone; but we might have to save our own lives by using guns, and the two outside can bring them in if they are needed."

"How can Hobbit keep from killing someone if he has to use that shotgun of his?" questioned Mary the woman. "Any where he hits someone will either kill them straight out or blow a leg or arm off, causing them to bleed to death. I wish we had all gotten shot-shells like Little Debbie."

Mary's last statement gave Hobbit an idea, and he solved the matter of the guns. "I will reduce the powder as well as the number of shot in my shotgun shells. And while I think about it, Gerterka will take care of the money. She can smell a stash of it six feet away. I'd leave the dope. When we leave we will call the police and tell them what has happened. They can get the dope and search the house for any more that might be there."

This plan pleased everyone, especially when they found out why Hobbit had been spending so much time with Gerterka the dog.

Everyone helped Hobbit reduce the load in his shotgun shells. There was an element of risk in reducing the shotgun shells, because the end of each shell had to be removed using a pocketknife. When the pellets poured out, a digging into the wadding holding the powder in had to be made; this was the really dangerous part. For this reason, everyone was patient, taking breaks to smoke or have a cup of coffee.

Soon, all was done and it was time to ride. The six, along with Gerterka, piled into the van. California Red drove. It was a long drive to the first house on the Gulf beach south of St. Petersburg, made even longer because they had to stay within the speed limit. They couldn't risk a bust for a speeding ticket, they had too many guns.

Instead of going into St. Pete and taking the toll bridge south, they turned down highway 41 and stayed on it until they got to the end of Tampa Bay. There they swung into the beach area of the Gulf of Mexico, heading to the dealer's house.

From the time they left Leesburg until they pulled up near the dope pusher's house the clock had moved two hours. Having the guns had slowed them down more than they had expected.

Red parked the van about a hundred yards from the house. There were lights on in the house. How may people were in the house would have to be determined by getting closer.

All of the six were armed with ether and terrycloth rags. Mary the woman and Screaming Girl took the point. After they had gotten to the side of the house, they began a slow, cautious move around it, peeking into windows as they did. As relatively small as the house was, it took them almost a half-hour to go around it. When they had finished their surveillance, they signaled to the others that there were two men and two women inside.

There was no voting now. The others waited on Hobbit to make the commands. They had trusted him with their lives before. This one would be the same.

Hobbit signaled to know if all four of the people were in the same room. The reply was "yes." He then signaled for the two women to go to the window of the room. The signals were hobo signs, as ancient as the original hobos of the 1920's who, in the western United States, had won the right of poor people to ride the rails. Many of them had been thrown off moving trains, their mangled bodies making food for whatever animals would eat them. After the stock market fell in nineteen twenty-nine, thousands more swelled the ranks of hobos until the railroads finally gave up. There were still a few young rail-yard workers who would call the law after a hobo; but most of them would not. They respected the rights of a people who lived such hard lives and were willing to fight just as hard.

When the women gave the signal that they were at the window, Hobbit told California Red and Mary the woman to go to the back door. He knew that Mary the woman had excellent hearing and, on that principle, he told her and Red to kick in the back door as soon as she heard him kick in the front door. None of them had guns with them.

Each of the six put on individual ski masks.

In minutes, everyone was in position and Hobbit, taking a running start, leaped into the front door with both feet. The door crashed open and all tarnation broke loose.

The two men inside grabbed lamps and swung them at Hobbit and Jack Frost. The two women fought and screamed. One of the men connected with a lamp and knocked Hobbit to the floor. Only after California Red and Mary the woman came into the room did the tide of battle change. But the six of them, somewhat bruised and battered, finally subdued the four with ether. While the others bound the four with clothesline, Hobbit went back to the van and got Gerterka. Inside, the dog smelled a stash right away, and Hobbit began tearing up an artificial tree in the living room. Sure enough, in the base of the tree was a substantial amount of money; from the looks of it, maybe a million dollars.

Earlier, Hobbit had ordered that none of them talk in the house except to interrogate, and he had a difficult time trying to tell them that he had found so much money. He had to give up on it, leaving Jack Frost and Mary the woman to interrogate the four people concerning the real Kingpin, while California Red and Little Debbie searched the rest of the house. He took Gerterka back to the van along with the money.

When he returned, California Red and Little Debbie were inside the broken front door, depositing what must have been a million dollars worth of cocaine. They left the cocaine just inside of the front door where the police could find it after they called them. In a pillowcase, California Red held a large assortment of jewelry. They had to wait a while longer for the four people to tell them what they wanted to know about the Kingpins. But, with that done, they went back to the van, removed their ski masks, and headed to Orlando, where they would call the cops and spend the night in a motel.

On the way to Orlando, Hobbit explained about the money. He told them he figured it to be close to a million dollars. He also explained that another major decision had to be made: should they take this money and run or should they take out the other dealer?

"How about the decision on whether or not to go after the real Kingpins?" Screaming Girl asked.

"Yeah," injected Jack Frost, "The one we got on to tonight lives in Miami, and he's stinking rich."

"What did ya'll use for stuff tonight," asked Hobbit.

"We used lighter fluid. It works better than anything else, and, if they won't talk, you can always set the lighter fluid on fire," Jack Frost told him.

After they had gotten three rooms in a motel on the northern side of Orlando, the six all converged in Hobbit's and Mary the woman's room to count the money. It took a long time, longer because the money had not been counted and wrapped according to denomination. Daylight was breaking when they arrived at a total: eight hundred and thirty-seven thousand dollars!

A hundred and thirty-nine thousand and five hundred dollars each! They had done it! They had hit the jackpot! Each used one of their pillowcases to put his or her money in. Later, they would get something more presentable. After claiming their money, they paired off and returned to their separate rooms for a much needed and well-deserved sleep.

When the maid knocked on the door, Hobbit put his clothes on and went to the office to pay for another day for all three rooms. He went back to his room and back to sleep.

It was middle afternoon before the six began waking. As they did, one from each room went to ask Hobbit what the plans were for the day. He told them that the best thing to do was to go back to Leesburg and leave most of the money in the shotgun house. With a fence around it and Sadie, Willie Mae, and their children close by, there was little chance anyone would break into it. Later, they could get bank deposit boxes like California Red's.

Everyone was still in a state of amazement over the money. None of them had ever seen that much before. California Red was very excited, too. He and Little Debbie now had close to three hundred thousand dollars and a third interest in the day care center.

When they arrived back in Leesburg, Jack Frost, who was in charge of the victory party, had Hobbit stop at a liquor store. He got a fifth of Jack Daniels and they proceeded to the shotgun house. They made one more stop. Fried chicken. Boxes of it! Jack Frost had already told them that he had some grass left from the last buy, and they all knew they would get the hungries.

While they were unloading the van, they saw Willie Mae and Sadie out in the yard of the day care center. That served as a reminder, and they began thinking of the two mothers, their children, and the others who worked there. The thinking overpowered Little Debbie and she stopped unloading. The others did the same.

"Are we all thinking about the same thing?" Little Debbie asked.

"You mean the two mothers?" questioned Mary the woman.

"Yes," she answered.

"We got real selfish all of a sudden," Screaming Girl added. "We ought to be thanking the Lord and thinking about ways to help others."

"Well, what do you think we should do?" spoke up California Red, "Go over there and give them some money?"

"No," interrupted Hobbit. "That would be the wrong thing to do. I was thinking on the way from Orlando that it would be a good idea to open another day care center. We could, along the same lines as this one, and that would allow one of the families to move out, giving both of them a lot of needed room. We might try to get something like we have here in the way of the shotgun house, too, because, if we stay to try the Kingpins, we are going to have to be around a while longer and this little house will get smaller by the day."

This brought on a general discussion, and, as it progressed in time, Jack Frost got up, poured six drinks of Jack Daniels and rolled two joints. After lighting up, he passed both the drinks and the joints around.

They never got rowdy; the marijuana took care of that: as for most alcoholics and ex-convicts who served long prison terms, grass served as a tranquilizer for all of them, but it was a good thing no one knocked on the door, because in two hours all of them were totally wrecked. When all of the chicken was finally eaten, and the meat off the bones of the leftovers given to Gerterka, they, one at a time, stretched out and went to sleep.

The first thing they did when they awoke the next morning was check their money to see if it was still there. It was, and all of them swore they would get a bank account and a bank deposit safe that very day. The thought that they had all passed out like they did, leaving the money totally unguarded, raised feelings of fear in them.

They finished unloading the van—the guns had been left there all night, and the gate was unlocked—then they began one by one to take quick showers and put on fresh clothes. When Gerterka was fed and put outside, they got their money and left, locking the gate behind them.

They went to different banks, all of them opening checking accounts for five thousand dollars each, then putting the rest in their safe deposit boxes. They had decided to look for a house or maybe two, but they felt safer with the money being kept in the bank. The previous night had been a loud and clear warning to all of them: they couldn't hold their whiskey and grass as well as they thought they could.

Each of them had kept several hundred dollars in their pockets, and Screaming Girl suggested they go over to Treasure Island and have a dip in the ocean.

"Let's go back and get Gerterka," Little Debbie told them. But Hobbit had something to say about that.

"I don't want anything to happen to that dog. It's too important."

"But you're making a prison out of her talent."

"It's not a talent," Hobbit insisted, somewhat perturbed. "I trained the dog. A Russian doctor named Pavlov wrote a book on it."

"And you read it in prison?"

"Yes! I read the thing in prison."

"Well, a tootie of a prisoner you must have been!"

"Have you ever been in prison?"

"No! And I won't ever be if I don't let some dumb bunny like you get me in one. And I'm not going to no darn beach. I'm staying home with Gerterka."

Hobbit backed down, and they went to the house and got Gerterka. The dog seemed very happy to ride in the van, and even happier when she got to the beach. Hobbit had to admit that Little Debbie was right. The dog was much more receptive to the commands the others were giving her, and that would make her even more valuable because she would not have to depend on him entirely to tell her what to do when they got to the Kingpin's house. He just hoped she didn't get too much salt in her nose.

They had a good time on the beach, and on the way back they discussed finding another house for a nursery. Their first option was to try the real estate sales person, Betty Cauldwell. In the meantime, they could look, too.

After they had talked with Betty Cauldwell over the phone, they went around to the day care center to tell the two mothers their plans.

"Oh, Gracious be," Willie Mae exclaimed. "I'm gonna give an extra five dollars at the church Sunday."

"You give five and I'll give five," spoke up Sadie.

"We'll let ya'll decide who moves after we get the house and fix it up; and we'll need your advice on that," Screaming Girl told them.

Both women said they would help all they could, and Willie Mae agreed to open the new nursery under her license. She also agreed to take further training in order to teach Sadie and the attendants enough to pass the certification test for a licensed child care person.

When the six walked back around the fence to get into the van, they let Gerterka out in the yard and locked the gate from the outside.

They drove all day, looking at house after house, but none suited them. When evening came, they gave up for the day, planning to call Betty Cauldwell the next morning.

The next morning, when Mary the woman went to the mail box to get the newspaper, she returned with that alarmed look on her face again. In huge letters on the top of the front page were the words "DRUG WAR RAGES. ONE DEAD." The story stated that a person suspected of being a major drug dealer had been killed and left bound along with three visitors in his home just north of Sarasota. There was no mention of finding the drugs. Police stated that they had been called by an anonymous person that a robbery had taken place at the house, and, when they arrived, they had found four people tied with clothesline, one of whom was dead from a gunshot wound to the head.

"We didn't do that," Little Debbie whispered tearfully. "There were no shots fired while we were there."

"I believe someone beat the police to the scene, found the dope inside the front door, which was half broken down, then went inside to take a further look," California Red suggested. "And the dealer recognized him, so he had to either kill the dealer or leave the dope."

"You're getting pretty good at this, Red," Hobbit complimented him.

"I'm just like Jack Frost," Red told him. "I'm in it all the way."

"I couldn't have gotten better news than that if I had paid for it," spoke Hobbit softly. He was much relieved. With California Red in, Little Debbie would certainly stay, and she might keep Screaming Girl in. He knew Mary the woman would stick with him. She wanted off the road. That was the bottom line for her, and having enough money to get off and stay off was the first prerequisite.

As had become common to them when matters became touchy, they took a vote. All agreed to stay in. With that done, they planned their day; looking for a day care house, mostly.

The next morning before the paper came, the phone rang and Betty Cauldwell told them she had found what just might be the ideal place for them. It was on the southwest side of Leesburg, going towards Tampa. She asked them to meet her there at eleven o'clock that morning.

Using the directions Betty had given them, they spotted her car just off the highway going to Tampa. When they pulled up in the yard, they knew immediately it was the right place. There were two houses on the property. One, a small bungalow, rested in the rear of the property much like the shotgun house on the other. The main house was two-storied, and when they looked inside they saw beautiful floors and woodwork again. They were fantastically pleased.

When they asked the price they were told it was two hundred and fifty thousand dollars, and a bargain at that.

They were stunned, first of all by the price, then by the fact that they had that much money to pay for it. When they had collected their wits, Hobbit spoke:

"We're going to have to look over it a little more, then talk to our financial backer. But we can let you know by tomorrow morning."

This satisfied Betty, and, after a few more social amenities, she left. When she was out of earshot, all of the six gave a big, loud "Spit" in unison.

"Whoever in the world ever heard of a bunch of tramps paying a quarter of a million dollars for anything?" Jack Frost exclaimed.

"Yeah," California Red agreed. "That's too much."

"I tell you what let's do right away," Hobbit told them. "Let's go back up town in Leesburg to the tax office and find out how much the place we have is valued. Then we will know how to figure on this matter."

Mary the woman smiled. She was glad she had drawn Hobbit. He was the leader because he had an educated intelligence. She agreed to his suggestion and the others followed her.

They were amazed when the tax office clerk told them that their property was assayed at two hundred thousand dollars. They then asked her if she could find the other property. She did. The last tax assessment appraised the two houses and lots at four hundred thousand dollars. The appraisal was so high because there were six lots on the property, all valued at forty thousand dollars each.

When they left the tax office, they felt as if they had become land barons. When they discussed it on the way back to the shotgun house, each one in turn made comments that exposed an elevated feeling of self-worth.

During their discussion, they estimated that they could get into the place and the business for just a little more than three hundred thousand. And it was a good investment. Not only would they have another business, they would have a higher credit line with which to buy another business, if they should so decide.

They decided to do it. With the hopes of Sadie and Willie Mae raised so high, there was nothing else to do. But no one complained that they should have kept their mouths shut. The big score was yet to come, and it wouldn't hurt if they spent all of their money.

Mary the woman called Betty Cauldwell early the next morning to tell her the decision had been made in favor of buying the houses and property. When the banks opened, each of them took fifty thousand dollars from their safe deposit boxes. By the end of the day, the houses and property were theirs.

Willie Mae and Sadie had already decided that Sadie would take the new place; so, as soon as the nursery was licensed, and all necessary work had been done on the house, Sadie and her children moved in.

The next day a full-page ad announced another Miracle Hill day care center. They had formed the new name for the purpose of advertising, thinking the name would draw new customers to the new house, and they were right: the first day twenty people called. By the end of the third day since opening, the nursery was full.

Hobbit and Mary the woman wanted to stay in the shotgun house, which left the bungalow to the other four. There were two bedrooms in the bungalow, a kitchen with bar opening into a dining room, living room, bath, and a screened-in front porch. California Red liked to sit out at night under the stars, and he was elated over the screened-in porch. At the shotgun house, he had to fight mosquitoes and all kinds of flying bugs for the space he occupied. There had to be something wrong with everything, and with Florida it was bugs.

When they discussed buying another vehicle, they settled on a mini-van. Hobbit told them to get a green one, because the color green was very hard to see at night, and they could use the van on the next score. No one had attempted to veto the hit on the dealer in Sarasota, so that was still on. They were simply waiting out the "drug war" in order to avoid running into a security ambush at the dealer's house.

They purchased a Chevrolet mini-van, sea green, six cylinders. It was comfortable, drove well, and had a good radio. To break it in, they drove down to Sarasota to check out the drug dealer's house. From what they could see, nothing special was going on. Perhaps the war was over.

The next day, the six checked the street dealers in Orlando, Tampa and St. Pete. Everything was cool. Business as usual.

"I think we had better stake out that house down in Sarasota," Hobbit told them. "They could have figured us out and be waiting with an ambush we can't see."

"Let's get car phones for both vans," Jack Frost suggested. "And we can get a cellular phone that one of us can carry around."

They agreed that the phones were a good idea and went to Radio Shack to get them. After they were installed, they drove from town to town testing the car phones, then took turns standing on street corners testing the cellular phone. Every one was happy with them. Soon, they started making plans to surveil the dealer's house again. This time, it would be an all-day job.

Mary the woman drew the first shift of watching the Sarasota dealer's house. Armed with binoculars and the cellular phone, she took up position the next morning at nine o'clock. Still sleepy, she guzzled coffee and smoked cigarettes to get herself awake.

At five that afternoon, Jack Frost relieved her.

At one o'clock in the morning, Hobbit relieved Jack Frost. Both vans and their two drivers had waited out on the beach, each anticipating a possible cellular phone call. At nine o'clock the next morning, California Red picked Hobbit up and they all headed back to Leesburg.

When the three lookouts compared notes, they came up with the conclusion that all activity that could be connected with drug traffic occurred during the day or early night. The six agreed on hitting the place the following Friday night after the drug transactions subsided. Ordinarily, most of the street dealers would buy their drugs for the weekend on that day, and Saturday was the usual party night for the suppliers.

When they rolled Friday afternoon, both vans were taken. Gerterka, who was still staying at the shotgun house, came with Hobbit and Mary the woman. She would be a busy little girl again before this night was over.

Not wanting to get to the house before dark, they stopped at a restaurant and had sandwiches for a late afternoon snack. The three women horsed around on the telephones, saying nothing in particular, but having a lot of fun. Finally, as the sun went down over the Gulf of Mexico, the drivers headed the two vans toward the dealer's house.

When they had parked, they opened the side doors and placed the telescopes in position. They had purchased them for just this occasion, and they were certainly in need of them now. There was no one at home in the dealer's house. This raised two serious questions: could it be a trap? And, if it wasn't a trap, should they enter the house and ambush whoever returned to it in order to get information on the Kingpin? The six of them convened between the two vans and five sets of eyes descended upon Hobbit.

Accepting his responsibility as leader of the group, Hobbit spoke. "I'll take the cellular phone and go down to the house. The ripping bar will go with me, too. Jack, you cover me with the shotgun. Red, if nothing happens, you bring Jack's pistol, and help me get into the house. If we get in and all is well, the rest of you bring ether, rags, and the rest of the guns. And Mary, you bring Gerterka."

With that done, Hobbit got the ripping bar out of the van and started walking to the house. He didn't hurry, and it took him several minutes to get to the carport. California Red walked a little faster. He motioned Hobbit out of the carport, and started making his way around the back side of the house. All of the windows had plexiglas on the outside, even the ones upstairs. They would have to go in through the back door.

When Hobbit caught up, Red motioned to the back door and gave a ripping sign. Hobbit put the wrecking bar in at the lock, pushed all of his weight behind the wrecking bar and gave it a snap. The door popped open with a dull bang. The two men stepped in and began reconning the house to make sure no one else was there before they signaled the others. Satisfied, they went upstairs and signaled out of the window. When they saw the others coming, California Red ran down to the front door and opened it just as the other four stepped up on the porch. Mary the woman put Gerterka down and scratched her money spot. She bounded up the stairs and in a minute was back, scratching on Mary's foot, the sign that she had located a stash of money. Mary started up the stairs, and Gerterka ran ahead of her. In the bedroom overlooking the back yard, Gerterka was scratching on the inside wall. The others were downstairs looking for dope and jewelry, so Mary had to go down to get Hobbit to bring the wrecking bar.

When he got to the bedroom and saw where Gerterka was scratching, he jammed the wrecking bar into the paneling and gave it a jerk backwards. A large section of the paneling came down. Behind it was a wall safe. It appeared to be a big one with a big combination lock. Hobbit signaled to Mary the woman to go down stairs and bring Jack Frost and California Red up. When she returned with them, he signed to them to tell him if they could open the safe. They signed "yes." Then both of them turned and ran downstairs out the door toward the vans. In minutes, they were running back, both carrying tools for cracking a safe; actually, for peeling a safe, and, while the others looked out for them, they began the noisy job of ripping the safe open. When they had ripped the front down to the tumblers, they dug into the rods and soon the safe door came open.

They were not at all prepared for what they saw. The safe was packed from bottom to top with packs of bills. When they tore down the first layer, they estimated that they saw a half a million dollars. They had forgotten to bring the duffel bag to put the money in, so Red and Jack took the bedspread off the bed and piled the money into it. Having emptied the safe, they rolled the spread up and carried it to the green van. While they stopped to smoke a cigarette, Hobbit, in the meantime, had gotten the duffel bag from the van and filled it with something from the house. Behind him came Mary the woman with a seat-cover full, and the other two women followed with something full of something. As Hobbit threw the duffel bag into the green van, he explained, "I decided to take the dope this time and we can pour it out later. At least no one will get killed over it that way."

Screaming Girl ran back to the house to get Gerterka, and turned the lights out. When she returned, Hobbit spoke again. "Now comes the really mean part of it. If we are going to get the information on this guy's supplier, we will have to wait inside the house until he gets back. We'll leave one person with the vans. I'll have the cellular phone if the van watcher needs us.

Hobbit decided on leaving Screaming Girl with the vans and Gerterka. He told the others to have a good smoke and return to the house. They were likely in for a long wait.

Then, putting on their ski masks, the five went back to the house.

It was almost three o'clock in the morning when a car pulled into the carport and people, laughing, cussing, and yelling, began getting out of it. The five inside couldn't tell how many were in the car, but, when they were satisfied that all of them were inside, Hobbit stepped out of the kitchen pantry with the shotgun. When the partiers stopped, somewhat stunned, the other four leaped upon them with ether rags. There were five of them, two men and three women. Hobbit handcuffed them in a circle because he didn't have enough handcuffs to do otherwise. He decided to concentrate on the two men, and, as the partiers began waking, he gave the three women another rag of ether and allowed the two men to fully waken. He liked the idea of using cigarette lighter fluid. It burned like blazes by itself, and if you set it on fire it really burned like blazes.

It didn't take very long for both of the men to become cooperative. As each of the five questioned them and became satisfied they were telling the truth, the women began waking. Since they had no further business there, the five left to go to the vans. They left the druggies handcuffed but conscious.

On the way back to Leesburg, things were pretty quiet. Hobbit had forbidden the use of the phones except in case of an emergency. Since Willie Mae was accustomed to hearing them coming in at all times, they went to the shotgun house to unload and inspect their booty.

They had found a suitcase full of jewelry downstairs. It was so much they didn't even bother to divide it, but just left it piled on the floor. The money came to one million six hundred and eighty-two thousand dollars, over two hundred and eighty thousand dollars each!

They had become so acclimatized to having money that they were not impressed with their new fortune. It still wasn't enough to get them off the road.

Having counted and divided the money, all of them relaxed, and, after a few minutes, fell asleep, their heads lying in their individual piles of green dollars.

They awakened around three o'clock that afternoon. All felt rum-dumb. Not until the second cup of coffee and three cigarettes did most of them start coming around. The first full-witted was Little Debbie.

"We need to do something about that dope. It's still in the van," she reminded them.

"We need to think of a good place to dump it," California Red said.

"I know," spoke up Jack Frost, "Let's take it down to alligator alley."

"No soap," Hobbit told them. "We will take it over to Jacksonville and put it in a dumpster. It should be cut up by the truck's cutter and distributed throughout the garbage, but, in case it doesn't work that way, no one will be able to trace it to any of the cities we deal with, and especially not Leesburg."

"Let's stay home until Monday," Screaming Girl proposed. "We can leave the dope here in the tan van. I want to stay close to this money until I can get it into a safe deposit box, and I sure don't want to lose it to some drug-sniffing dog on the highway."

Her last statement caused a shudder of fright to run through the others. It was the first time they had considered the thought of losing the money and going to jail for possession of drugs.

"I tell you what," Hobbit spoke again, "Red, you take the green van to the hardware store and buy us some shovels. And stop by that feed and seed store and get some of those big plants. We'll dig a big hole, bury the dope in it, and plant the things on top of it."

"But what about us, Hobbit," Mary the woman asked. "Suppose a policeman with a drug-sniffing dog drives by here?"

"Alright," answered Hobbit. "We will dig the holes now. Tonight, we will tear the packs of dope open and pour the stuff in the hole. Then, we will pour gasoline over the dope and set it on fire. After that, we can pour cayenne pepper over it, and we can still put the plants over the whole thing."

The others thought this over and decided they would do it.

While California Red was gone to get the shovels and plants, Little Debbie put her and Red's money into two separate leaf bags she found under the sink in the kitchen.

There were more bags left, and the others followed Little Debbie's lead.

When Red returned, he brought three shovels, and they began digging a trench, taking turns with the digging. Because the ground was so moist, they had to dig wider and longer than usual in order to compensate for the walls caving in, but, after a little more than an hour, they had a respectable trench dug, and all stopped to take a break.

As they sat on the grass in the back yard, a police car came by. Hobbit waved at the officer, and he waved back. When the policeman had passed, he told the others, "We had better burn that dope right now. If that guy had a drug-sniffing dog, we would be in a lot of trouble."

The three women went to the van, brought the dope to the trench and threw it in. Jack Frost had gotten the extra gallon of gas from the back of the green van. He poured it on the dope and everyone smoking flipped their cigarettes into the hole. It burst into a roaring flame, and all of the six jumped back from the trench, then walked back into the house.

"Do you know what we just did," California Red puzzled to them. "We just free based over a million dollars worth of cocaine."

Jack Frost laughed. "I guess there will be some high birds around here tonight," he cackled.

Each of the six had gotten a small whiff of the cocaine fumes and they were on an upper high. When the euphoria wore down, they went to the window to see if the job had been done. It had, and they felt safe to venture back into the yard, but the ashes were still smoldering and they went around the house to the front yard.

Happily, they saw that Willie Mae and her kids were not at home. No one had thought of them, and it was a sad thought to recognize so late, but at least it wasn't too late this time. It would serve as a lesson for the future. They reentered the house through the front door, and Mary the woman went to the back porch to turn the outside light on. Having done this, first she got the cayenne pepper to pour over the burned dope; then she went outside and began placing the plants in an orderly line down the trench. That done, she began covering the plants' roots with dirt. Within an hour, she had finished her task, and she went back inside the house. At least she would sleep better that night knowing the dope was gone.

Everyone agreed on beer and pizza for dinner that evening, and California Red offered to go and get it. Hobbit said he would go with Red to keep him company.

When they had gotten the beer and pizza and were headed back to the shotgun house, Hobbit asked California Red if he was still in for the big score.

"I am willing to stay around to see what it is going to look like."

"It's going to look so good you will never live it down if you don't stay in."

"How do you figure that?"

"By the money we have gotten off these little guys. The Kingpins are making so much money you can't even imagine it."

"I'll talk it over with Little Debbie. She's all hot to go to California, get married and open a restaurant."

"You don't have enough money to buy a car, a home, and open a restaurant."

California Red thought for a minute, then nodded. "Yeah," he said. "I guess you're right." Hobbit was sure that if California Red and Little

Debbie stayed in, the rest would too, and, if all stayed in, the big score would be a real possibility.

As soon as everyone had gotten well into the pizza and beer, Hobbit again brought up the subject of the big score. He reminded them that he was their leader, and their current success should count a lot toward staying with him. He also pointed to the fact that he hadn't taken any unnecessary risks.

"What if the big one proves to be too risky?" Little Debbie asked. "Are you still going to try it?" "No," he answered her, "If we can't do it, we can't do it; so I'll back off."

"I'm with Hobbit," California Red spoke up. "He has led us this far without a serious incident, and I am for staying with him on this thing."

Hobbit acknowledged his thanks.

"I said from the beginning that I was in it all the way," stated Jack Frost.

Mary the woman said she would follow Hobbit, and Screaming Girl acknowledged that she was still in, also.

Satisfied, Hobbit allowed the subject to drop.

"We need to buy Sadie and Willie Mae a couple of good used cars, Screaming Girl told them. They have really been doing a great job, and now that we can afford it we need to give them something extra."

The other two women seconded the idea and Hobbit broke the possible tie. Monday morning, as soon as they had put most of their money in a safe deposit box, they would go car shopping. They decided to take the green van in order for all of them to be able to see out of the windows, an accommodation the golden tan van did not have.

They had been to several car lots, finding nothing suitable, when the women gave a shrill "Stop!"

The objects of their attention were two Saturn automobiles on a small car lot that they almost passed by. They were certain that if everything checked out mechanically these would be the right cars.

They checked out fine and, when they told the salesman that they would pay cash, he came down a hundred on each car. All of the six were pleased with their decision.

Before they left town to deliver the cars, they stopped by the Mission's day care center and each of them made a one thousand-dollar contribution. They all also resolved to attend the evening Bible studies and all church services held that week before beginning to work on the plans for the big score.

Willie Mae was the first one to receive one of the Saturns, and she hollered like a choir singer. Screaming Girl gave her an additional five hundred dollars to pay for insurance and registering the car. Little Debbie cried for the joy Willie Mae experienced, and Mary the woman determined to get in on giving Sadie her car. All of the children came, and, as soon as they understood that the car now belonged to their mother, they began climbing in the seats and in and out of the doors. Willie Mae said that since the car was full, she might as well take it for a ride. California Red laughed and gave her fifty dollars for pizzas. When they pulled into the front yard of the new day care center, Sadie came out on the porch, wondering what this new action could imply, but, when she saw the smiles on their faces, her fears were immediately quelled, for she knew that none of the six ever tried to fool her. But she was totally unprepared for what was going on, and, when she found out, she began screaming at the top of her voice and ran to the car. Screaming Girl, who had been driving, jumped out of the car and Sadie jumped in. The five children, who had been watching from an upstairs window, came running down the staircase into the yard and jumped into the car. They jumped up and down in the seats so hard that Sadie had to scold them.

Mary the woman presented the papers for the car to Sadie, and gave her six hundred dollars, telling her that the money was for registration, insurance and pizzas.

As Sadie drove off with her children, the six got back in their van and headed for the shotgun house for a little fellowship. They had not spent any real quiet time together since they started hitting the drug dealers. It was time for a break.

Mary commented on the birds playing in the bushes she had planted. She had thrown birdseed around them, and was happy that her idea had worked.

"Hobbit," she asked, "Do you think we will have to kill anyone this time? After all, these are Kingpins. They're smarter than the others."

"If it looks like it will for certain go that far, we won't do it. I have a value for human life, too, and what they are doing has not been made a capital crime."

"I'm glad you feel that way, Hobbit," she continued, "And I'm just as sure that the others are. They all have more money than they ever hoped to have in their lifetime. It won't disappoint them to not get any more. You've done a great job of being our leader, and they know that, too."

"What are you going to do, Mary, if we make the big score?"

"Make it or not, I'm going to Aspen, Colorado, and open a beauty shop. I was a registered cosmetologist at one time, and I can re-certify. That and a little money is all I need.

"I'm kind of thinking that I will stay here and run these day care centers, maybe open another one or two, depending on the money."

"Are you thinking about still going to church? I've been thinking about it."

"I've been thinking about it, too. Seems to be a good time to start thinking about the other side. We are only born once, and we only die once. Nothing we could do about the first. About the second, well, some call it hope, some call it faith; and I guess everyone wants to live in a hereafter."

When the other four agreed to attend evening Bible lessons at the Mission, the talk soon subsided and California Red said it was time for them to go home to their bungalow. After they had gone, Mary threw two pork chops into a frying pan and put them on the stove. Hobbit started some water to boil for instant potatoes, then reached into the refrigerator for a cold bottle of vin rose. In a few minutes, they were eating.

The Bible lesson that night was good. It was about Solomon using unbelievers to build God's temple. The six felt like the message was made just for them, and they were more and more confident that it was God's will for them to rob the Kingpin drug dealers. They also felt more conscience-free about the dealers they had already robbed.

All of the evening Bible lessons at the Mission went well; likewise, the Wednesday evening church service. When Sunday morning came around, they all put on their best clothes and sat up front in the church. The sermon was about giving yourself wholly to the Lord, and Screaming Girl was so touched by it she said she was actually considering going back that night and taking a nose-dive. Hobbit talked her out of it, at least until after the big score.

Monday morning, they were all packed up and headed for Miami. Excitement sparked the air in both vans, and the women kept the telephones going most of the time.

When they arrived in Miami, they went to the western side and rented motel rooms for the night. They planned to go apartment hunting the next day. They would need one furnished for maybe two months. All had agreed not to approach this Kingpin thing without caution.

It took two days to find an apartment, and it wasn't all that good, but it did have air conditioning.

The next day, they went Kingpin hunting. Based on the directions they had obtained from the other drug persons, the homes of both dealers were west of Miami. When they arrived at the first one, they were flabbergasted. It was a mansion! And it had dogs almost as big as the alligator they had met on the rode that night. Men in short-sleeved shirts walked around with pistols on their hips. In the front was an iron gate. A high cyclone fence ran around the property. Hobbit called California Red, who was driving the green van, and told him to wait. He began driving around the property.

There was another gate in the rear. From the looks of it, less ornamental than the front, it was the service gate. After he had seen this, he speeded up, told Mary to call Red to get ready to leave, then, when he came back around to the front, they headed back toward Miami.

Instead of stopping at a restaurant, Hobbit told them that they would buy groceries and eat at home. They had a lot to talk about, and a restaurant was too risky.

While the women cooked the meal, the three men sat around the breakfast table.

"We only have one chance," Hobbit told them.

"Well," exclaimed Jack Frost, "That is one big improvement. I didn't think we had a chance of a snowball in the hot place."

"We might not," Hobbit admitted, "but it's worth putting some time into, and it will take time."

"Do you think we should call Sadie and Willie Mae?" Little Debbie asked.

"I thought you had already told them we would be here for two months."

"I did, but I just wanted them to know."

"We'll call them if we take any longer."

While they ate, Hobbit outlined the plan. First, they would go and look over the other drug Kingpin's house. Logically, it would be along the same lines as the first one. If so, they would begin watching them with the telescopes as far away from the houses as possible. Every time they was a major move of people, they would follow them. The point was to find out where they were going when a lot of them went.

That night they went out to the other Kingpin's house. It was almost a replica of the first, also having a back gate service entrance.

"We need to figure out how we can watch both houses and the four entrances at the same time," Hobbit told them. "I'm beginning to believe that both of them work together; so when one moves, the other moves with him."

Jack Frost offered an idea. "If we got two more telescopes, we could stake out the other side with a person not in a vehicle."

"The problem with that is that we are only six people and have only two vehicles," Mary the woman spoke up. "We can buy another vehicle, but no more people, and it would take four people at a time to watch the two houses. I think a two-person stake-out is a good idea, but for just one house at a time."

They tossed around a few more ideas, but finally settled on Mary the woman's suggestion. They would take one house at a time, beginning with the first one. The shifts would run eight hours each, three shifts a day, every day. Playtime was over. It was time to go to work.

They decided to stay in pairs in order that the partners would have some time together, and Jack Frost and Screaming Girl drew the first shift. They agreed between themselves to swap stations from day-to-day, and, at eight o'clock the next morning Screaming Girl dropped Jack Frost off about three hundred yards from the rear of the house. They had brought the telescope that had been in the golden tan van for the back way watcher to use.

At two o'clock that afternoon Hobbit and Mary the woman showed up in hunting fatigues. They had also brought a cellular phone in order to communicate with each other. The absence of the phone with the first two watchers worried Hobbit. It was a mistake. If the back watcher had spotted anything, he would have had to wait until the shift was over to report it. In their proximity to the drug Kingpin's house, a mistake could cost some of them their lives.

Ten o'clock rolled around uneventfully, and California Red and Little Debbie relieved them. They, too, had on hunting fatigues and asked for the cellular phone. Debbie told Mary that the other two realized the mistakes they had made that morning and were out buying fatigues.

As the days rolled past, the six remained patient but discouraged. They didn't get to do anything anymore. The six of them could never be together, and both vans were tied up at all times, one at the site, the other on call. They were scared to take a drink. Scared they might make a mistake and get themselves killed. There was nothing to do but work.

Hobbit and Mary the woman had agreed to change watch places from day-to-day also, and it was Mary the woman who called in the movement. She had three-way calling, and she told the other five that it looked like everyone but the dogs were piled into six Cadillacs.

Hobbit pulled out immediately. When he got to the spot where Mary was she jumped into the van and pointed in the direction of the cars. They were headed toward southwest Florida.

Mary stayed in touch with the other four by car telephone. She gave them directions, and, in about an hour, they caught up with them. They allowed the motorcade to stay well ahead of them in order not to arouse suspicion.

Almost as soon as the others caught up with them, the motorcade turned into the Everglades National Park. After considerable winding around, they stopped. Hobbit told Mary to advise Red to follow him closely because he planned to drive right past the drug dealers. He did, and they saw the crowd of men getting into airboats.

They were obviously going out to one of the many small islands, and there was no way they could watch them by land. There certainly were no hills: the highest elevation in Florida is only a few hundred feet high.

When they had driven past them far enough not to be seen, they stopped and cut off their engines. Then when they heard the boat engines start, they started to crank up and go back to Miami. But a fantastic thing occurred. Another motorcade appeared to be coming through the glades. They watched, thinking it might be law enforcement officers, but it wasn't. It was another motorcade just like the one that had just gotten into the boats. In a few minutes, these, too, got into boats and started in the same direction the others had gone. Led by Hobbit, the six got out of the vans and walked to the spot where the cars were. No one was in the cars. No one was watching.

In the meantime, the six watched and waited. When they saw an airplane's lights going down as if for a landing in the direction the boats had gone, they all ran to the vans and got on top, trying to see where the location was. No soap. But they did have a pretty good idea.

An hour later, they heard the sound of boats coming back. They walked back to the vans, and hid in the bushes where they could see the boats unload. Their eyes had become accustomed to the night light, and they saw for the first time that the men getting out of the boats were armed with automatic weapons. They also observed that all of these men began walking around the perimeter. Three of them began walking in the direction of the vans. None of the six had brought their guns, and they would have been very short of fire power anyway; so they lay in the bushes, hoping they would not be seen.

Happily, before they reached the curve in the road around which they could have seen the vans, the three gunmen turned around. One of them said something in Spanish and the others laughed.

In a few minutes, more boats were heard. This time, there was a lot of activity. Trunks were opened. Packages were placed in the trunks. There was a general inspection of the boats, then the first motorcade left. Thirty minutes later, the second one left.

When they could no longer see the lights of the last motorcade, Mary the woman and Little Debbie, who were now driving, waited just a few additional minutes, then started driving out the road that led from the Everglades. When she spotted a small restaurant ahead, Mary told Hobbit to call Debbie and tell her she was stopping for coffee.

They got the coffee to go and took it outside where they congregated around the green van.

"Who believes they picked up a load of dope?" Jack Frost said, laughing.

The other five laughed with him, and agreed that they had just witnessed the two ends of a major drug transaction. Now, the question was, did they pay for the drugs when they got them? They decided to leave that question on the burner for a few days. Since there surely would be no drug buys in the Everglades for some time, the six felt that they could take a break from house watching. They did, and the next morning all headed for the beach.

After a week of spending every day at the beach, the dull edges of their lives were sharpened. They were ready to go back to work again.

When the shifts began the next day, they didn't notice anything different from the previous month. They did, however, observe that as the month wore on activity around the house lessened. They assumed that this meant the Kingpin had distributed his dope to the intermediate dealers.

As the twenty-fifth of the month approached—the date of the last major movement—anticipation filled the six with excitement. If the motorcade moved on or within a few days of the twenty-fifth, this would be the last of the dry runs. The next run next month would be the real thing.

On the twenty-eighth the motorcade moved.

Mary the woman again spotted the movement and called Hobbit. He in turn called the others.

Mary the woman had made a closer observation this time. She reported that there were the same six Cadillacs, and added that each car held four men. All were armed with automatic weapons, and, with the exception of one, all deposited a small suitcase into the trunk of the car they rode in.

Hobbit led point again, and the events occurred just as they had the previous month. There were two motorcades, four boats, one plane, and the six experienced the same fear as they had previously when the three armed men walked in their direction checking the perimeter.

One additional thing they noticed: there were four men in each car of the second motorcade, all armed with automatic weapons, and, with the exception of one, each deposited a small suitcase into the car they rode in.

"Hobbit," Jack Frost spoke up," Do you know we are thinking about going up against forty-eight men armed with Uzis?"

"You were in the army?" Hobbit asked him. "Yes, I was," he answered. "Then you're elected," Hobbit told him.

"Elected to what?"

"Tell you in the morning."

When they awoke refreshed and alert the next morning, the six had breakfast in the apartment. Over a second cup of coffee, the others began prodding Hobbit for information on the next move. "First of all," he began, "I'll answer Jack's question. I want you, Jack, to find an active army quartermaster who likes money. We will need a lot of stuff. He can get the stuff and write it up as cannibalized, old equipment used for parts, and there will be no problem."

"Like, for instance, what are we going to need from an army quartermaster?"

"Tear gas canisters and launchers, gas masks, and air tanks."

"How many of each?"

"I figure forty-eight tear gas canisters and the same number of launchers. One for each of us on the gas masks and oxygen tanks."

"Now, Screaming Girl," Hobbit continued, "Since you and Jack will be working together, you get us five gallons of ether, two large terry cloth towels and a large box of freezer bags. When you get all of this stuff, all of us will help put it together."

"Red, you and Little Debbie get all of us either green or fatigue jump suits. They need to be lightweight. I don't want to die of heat exhaustion waiting on those people to show up." He and Mary the woman would shop for canned goods, bread and drinks that they could carry on to the island. The next day, Screaming Girl had the ether and bags. Jack Frost said he had a lead on a quartermaster, but he would have to go to Columbus, Georgia to make contact. Hobbit told him to go. He also told everyone else to come up with ten thousand dollars each and give it to Jack Frost.

"And if you can come up with an M16 and a case of shells, you've got yourself a gun," he told Jack Frost. "We could use one on the plane, and you're the only one experienced with an M16."

After Jack and Screaming Girl left, Hobbit put the others to helping with the ether. He cut the two terry cloth towels into strips, then into pieces about an inch square. These went inside the baggies, three pieces to a bag. When this was done, ether was dipped from the five-gallon drum and a full cup poured into each plastic bag. The zip lock was then fastened securely. The finished bags were boxed and placed in a cool closet to await the departure of the six to the Everglades.

California Red and Little Debbie had gotten the fatigues, and the sizes were fine. The four had suits to fit them, and the remaining two looked like they would fit Jack Frost and Screaming Girl excellently.

Hobbit asked Little Debbie to call Sadie and Willie Mae to tell them that they would be down there another month; also, to ask about Gerterka.

Two weeks later, Jack Frost called, saying he had everything that had been ordered plus a couple of extra items. He expected to be in Miami in two days.

Gerterka was doing fine, living in the house with Sadie and her kids. The kids had really taken up with the dog, and would be saddened when it had to return to the shotgun house. Hobbit made a mental note to stop on the way back to Leesburg and buy the kids a dog, a small one like Gerterka.

As soon as Jack Frost and Screaming Girl got back, the six went into the Everglades and rented a boat. It took awhile and a few wet feet to find it, but they finally found the island with the landing strip. When they returned to the small marina, Hobbit asked the owner if he ever rented boats for long periods of time. He said he rented to anyone with money for as long as they could pay. There was no other way out of this area of the Everglades unless you went out to sea, so he wasn't worried about getting his boat back.

Hobbit told him that they would be back on the twenty-first of the month, and would need three airboats to carry them, their food and photographic equipment. Hobbit explained that they were taking pictures for National Geographic.

When they returned on the twenty-first, they paid the marina owner for two weeks in advance and asked him if, after they unloaded them, could he park their vans in a safe place.

The owner told them that they could park them at his house, which was about two hundred yards further around the curve you could see going into the Everglades. This pleased them, because they were familiar with the curve, and didn't expect any of the men to go past it looking for anything.

After they had loaded their equipment, which included some obvious cameras with tripods, Jack Frost and California Red drove the two vans up to the marina owner's house and walked back. As soon as they boarded the boats, Hobbit took the lead, and the three airboats were on their way.

Getting set up on the island took some time. They circled it several times in order to find a place that the drug Kingpin's boats would not enter from. Then they had to locate the place where they did enter.

They pulled their boats into the western side of the island. They didn't unload. It would take the rest of the day to recon the island; then they would unload.

Night fell gently over the Everglades. The bright moon created a romantic overture with the aid of birds, bugs, and an occasional grunt from an alligator. They were especially careful of alligators. Gators were night hunters.

All of the six elected to sleep in the boats that night, and odd-man-outs determined who would take which of the six two-hour watches.

Not since their train days had they eaten out of cans, thus the experience brought back forgotten memories. Some of them were so filled with nostalgia they brought tears to the eyes of the rail tramps turned mercenaries.

"It's a good thing we didn't bring any wine with us," commented Hobbit. "If we had, we would all pack it up and go back to the rail yard."

"I hope this is the last time I ever do anything like this," Screaming Girl added. "I wanted off the road, but this is getting to be too much for me."

"Me, too," said Little Debbie.

Mary the woman held her peace. Neither of the other women knew what it was really like to be on the road, but she did, and she would lay out in the Everglades with alligators and kill every drug dealer anywhere to get off of it.

All of them began waking at daybreak the next morning and were greeted with a tin cup, a roll of toilet paper and a bottle of Coca Cola. The idea was to pour the Coke in the tin cup, roll up some of the toilet paper, set it on fire and hold the cup over the fire until it heated the Coke. It took a little doing, but everyone managed to survive the first session with a cup of hot Coke. For food, they had vienna sausages and bread. They didn't want to risk the odor of a Coleman stove.

As soon as they had eaten and had a second cup of hot Coke, Hobbit began assigning each of them to tasks. Jack Frost he assigned to setting out the tear gas launchers. He told Screaming Girl to place ample canisters of tear gas beside each launcher. Jack recommended five. California Red, Little Debbie, and Mary the woman were put to setting out the ether bags. They placed five of them between each tear gas launcher station in order to not get them mixed up. The explosion of the tear gas canisters could ignite the ether, and that they didn't want.

Hobbit cleaned up the area where they had eaten. He didn't want to invite an alligator to supper, and he didn't want one of the Kingpin guards to spot a camping ground. When he had finished, he put the extra things back into an air boat. He stood for a minute to ponder the air boat. It was a wide boat with a flat shallow hull that had a huge window fan mounted on the back, driven by a gasoline motor. It must have taken a real genius to figure out something as simple as that, because lesser minds always made things complicated.

When all had completed their tasks, they congregated around Hobbit, each lighting up a cigarette.

"Now, that's another thing," Hobbit began. "You must bury your cigarette butts in the dirt on our side of the island. We can't take any chances with anything that will give us away. We are going to have to train ourselves to launch the canisters, then throw the ether bags. We will train with unloaded launchers and handfuls of dirt."

Hobbit showed Jack Frost what he had in mind, and Jack began training the others. The idea was simple. Of the five, three would take up a station that would require them to fire ten teargas launchers respectively; two would fire nine each. After they trained that day, they would arm each launcher. Later at action time, when all of the teargas canisters had been fired, they would each begin lobbing ether bags into the melee of men.

Jack Frost would keep the M16 near him, and, if anything seriously went wrong, he would fire a tracer bullet into the ether bags.

"I thought we weren't going to kill anybody," Screaming Girl spoke up.

"We might have to make a choice between ourselves and a bunch of drug dealers," Hobbit explained. "No one wants to have to make that choice, but it might come to that."

Everyone remained quiet for a minute; then Jack Frost rallied them for the training exercises.

Things went slowly at first, but they sped up little by little. Soon, all were acquitting themselves like experts.

They broke off for lunch, going to the boats to make sandwiches of Spam. This time, they had lukewarm Coke, but they were hungry and it didn't matter.

When asked about the footprints behind the launchers, Hobbit told them that if the drug henchmen could see the footprints, they could see the launchers. He, however, would be down by the water where they landed, and would shoot holes in the bottoms of the drug dealers' boats. In case of an early emergency each of them should fire a tear gas launcher, throw an ether bag and run for their boats. There were many small islands that would provide them with protection from the drug Kingpins' firepower.

They spent the rest of the afternoon going over their training maneuvers. Hobbit found a place near the dope dealers' landing spot to hide his shotgun. Jack Frost took the middle launcher, because he wanted to take a shot at the plane's motors when it landed. When evening began pulling a thin blanket of darkness over the island, the six went about loading the teargas launchers. That done, they went to the boats and had supper. This time, they ate canned soup out of the can and made peanut butter sandwiches.

The next day was pretty much a replica of the first, except they unloaded the tear gas launchers before practice.

When Mary the woman asked about the handfuls of dirt they were throwing toward the landing strip, Hobbit told her it would be all right. The wind became very strong in the Everglades sometimes, so anything relative to the Glades would go unnoticed. These people had been at this for a long time; they wouldn't get excited about a little dirt strewn around.

That night Hobbit recommended that everyone sleep as much as they could. The next morning, each person would begin taking two-hour watches during the day. The watches would continue into the night.

As the long, eventful-less nights wore on, discouragement invaded the group. Their attitudes became negative; their relationships with each other bordered on hostility. Everyone, even Hobbit, cursed the food.

Then, on the twenty-seventh day of the month at ten PM they heard the sound of boats approaching. Each of the six ran hurriedly to their places. They were ready.

The first convoy of boats landed, bringing twenty-four men with visible guns and twenty-three of them carrying small suitcases. As the first ones made their vessels secure, the sound of more boats could be heard in the distance. The twenty-four men waited at the landing place to assist the men coming in from the other boats. When their boats were secured, the forty-eight armed men, forty-six of whom were carrying additional suitcases, proceeded to the front of the landing strip.

The six had their gas masks on and their air tanks nearby. The air tanks were for emergency use in case their gas masks failed.

Soon, the groan of the twin-engine plane could be heard, and, very shortly, its landing lights appeared.

The landing lights were the signal the six had agreed upon. Each one fired the tear gas launcher in front of them, and ran to the next one in their line. As the canisters exploded, Hobbit began shooting double-ought buck shot into the hulls of the Kingpins' airboats.

Just as the five began throwing the ether bags into the gassed and gurgling men, the plane began its approach for landing; but, when the pilot saw what was happening, he lifted the nose of the plane to abort the landing. When Jack Frost saw that, he swung the M16 around to his shoulder and began firing at the right motor. It worked. The motor went dead and the plane began limping. He wouldn't get far, and he would probably have to bail out and let the plane crash.

The drug Kingpins and their guards began passing out, some falling on top of each other. Just as the last one dropped to the ground, Hobbit ran out and started picking up Uzis. He signaled to the others to do likewise. His principle in doing this was that if any of the men revived before they got away, they wouldn't have any fire power with which to harm the six. When the guns were loaded on the boats, Hobbit signaled to start picking up the suitcases. As small as they were, they were heavy, and even Hobbit, with his huge hands, had trouble carrying more than four at a time. The men eventually felt the weight of the suitcases and began carrying only two. The women went down to one.

With the cases on board, they turned to Hobbit for instructions about the teargas launchers.

"Leave 'em," he told them. "If we ever need anything like that again, I'll go back on the road."

California Red took a message from Hobbit's last remark, and opened his knife. Then he began to pry open one of the suitcases. When he opened it, he said, "You won't have to worry about needing any more teargas launchers if the rest are like this one. It's full of one hundred dollar bills."

"My God!" exclaimed Mary the woman. "Let's get out of here fast. With all the noise we made, along with the plane motor being shot off, this area will be crawling with law enforcement officers very shortly."

The others agreed and began shoving the boat off.

As they motored back to the marina, Hobbit began throwing the drug dealers' guns overboard. The others did likewise, and soon all of the guns were in the bottom of the Everglades.

When they returned to the marina, California Red and Jack Frost ran up the road the get the vans. Returning, they reported that the people in the house were up and around, but did not come out to greet them. There actually was no need for them to, since the airboats did not have ignition keys, and they were still paid up for a full week in advance. But Hobbit said he didn't like the looks of things, and they might have a problem trying to keep the vans. If the marina owners took down their tag numbers, they would for certain turn them over to the feds.

They needed to get back home, count the money and divide it; then go their separate ways. Hobbit said he would stay and take the heat, if there was any. Both of the vans were registered in his name, so running would not do any good for him.

The suitcases were loaded on the two vans, and the six began the half-hour drive out of the Everglades. Every flicker of light was frightening. If the cops caught them with as much money as they had, they would never make them believe they were not rival drug lords. The fear was so intense the five smokers didn't even light up a cigarette.

They made it out of the Everglades without incident, and all of the smokers lit up. Just as they did, they rounded a bend in the road and saw, less than a quarter of a mile away in an open field, a kaleidoscope of lights—red, blue, yellow and white—all flashing. The lights were attached to law enforcement vehicles. In the center of them was an airplane with one motor gone. The six didn't care about verifying their suspicions; they just wanted out of there in a real hurry.

On the outskirts of Miami, Hobbit turned his van toward the interstate going north. It would be at least a three-hour drive back to Leesburg. With the van tanks full of gas, he didn't plan on stopping until he pulled up to the gate at the shotgun house. Even when the others in the van behind him wanted to stop for coffee, he vetoed it. This was the big score, and he didn't want to lose it because of some flukey thing happening. The sooner they divided the money and split up, the better off they would be.

Daylight shone over Leesburg when the six pulled up to the shotgun house. After unlocking the gate, driving the vans in and locking the gate back, the six carried the money into the party room of the house.

Little Debbie and Screaming Girl grabbed the instant coffee and ran cups of hot water from the faucet. As soon as they got their first cup down, they made another in the same fashion, but put it into the microwave to heat it up more. California Red had put a pot of hot water on the stove. As soon as it boiled, he made coffee for Mary the woman, himself, Hobbit, and Jack Frost.

Screaming Girl, her nerves settled down, asked, "How are we going to count this money?"

"We can count one case and divide on the basis of that one," responded Hobbit. "Or we can think about taking all day and count all of it."

"Let's count one," suggested Jack Frost, "then dump the others out one at a time to see if they look alike. If all the piles look alike, we can divide on the basis of the one we counted."

Hobbit was the first to second the motion on Jack Frost's suggestion, and no one spoke to the contrary.

There were two hundred and fifty thousand dollars in the suitcase they counted. Pouring the rest of them out on the floor in separate piles proved that all of them looked alike. This was certainly the big score. Eleven million, five hundred thousand dollars! Almost two million dollars each!

"The shares come to one million, nine hundred sixteen thousand and six hundred and sixty-six dollars," Hobbit told them. "We'll buy Gerterka some of those dog bones she likes with the change."

Gerterka had heard them laughing and talking, and she started barking. At first, she barked only a little bit, then quit. But her quits became fewer and fewer; so Hobbit told Mary the woman to go around to Sadie's house and bring the dog home. She did, and, very shortly, Gerterka was shaking and jumping around in the shotgun house so much that if she were a bigger dog she would have shattered the glass in the windows. Each of the six patted her on the head and said something nice to her.

The next morning, they had to rent additional safe deposit boxes, and that became a clandestine effort. They had too much money. First, each of them had to take about a quarter of a million dollars, such as could be disguised in one's clothes, and deposit it into the newly-rented box. Then, each of them had to make additional trips with the same amount of money, and deposit it into the same box. Since this was going to cause each of them to make eight trips to the same bank, they had first to be sure they got different banks.

That done, the first two trips were easy. The bank teller in charge of the safe deposit boxes smiled through both of them; but the third and thereafter trips were met with cool to cold frowns. Finally, as the afternoon drew to an end, Jack Frost suggested that they each keep a hundred thousand dollars and raise the amount they were stuffing in their pockets. This worked out well, and they finished the job with only seven trips. The people at the banks certainly suspected something, but they were off balance enough to not know exactly what was going on. As Hobbit often said, "Keep them off balance, and you remain in control."

When they had deposited their money, Jack Frost wanted to buy a car. A red convertible, he said.

California Red was driving the green van, and he pulled into a Ford dealership. Almost immediately Jack Frost fell in love. Sitting majestically in the center of the showroom floor was the most beautiful red Ford Mustang in the world. He didn't even ask to try it out. He just told the salesman to draw up the papers.

The salesman's eyes bulged when Jack Frost counted out twenty thousand dollars in cash, and he was smiling all over himself. He wouldn't have to wait on his commission on this one!

As Jack turned into the street from the dealership, Hobbit told California Red to go by the Saturn place. Not where they had bought the two used ones, the new-car Saturn dealership. This time, Hobbit turned out into the street driving a new car, and Jack Frost offered to race him. Hobbit declined, and the six returned to the shotgun house.

While Mary the woman unlocked the gate to the back of the house, Gerterka greeted her with a friendly bark, and she remembered that they had not gotten the dog biscuits. She hollered to Hobbit, told him, and he left to get them. When he returned, Gerterka had a fit over the biscuits. She ate half of a box—full before Mary the woman took them away from her. "Darn dog will kill itself eating," she said.

Hobbit left again, returning with a small dog he had gotten from the animal shelter. It was for the kids.

As previously agreed, after they had showered, shaved, perfumed and changed clothes, they all met later that evening at the Red Lobster in Tampa. The vans were left at the shotgun house. Hobbit and Jack Frost had driven their cars.

They got a table for six, and, after ordering, began discussing the future state of affairs. It was decided that Hobbit would have full title to the nursery buildings and property as well as the two vans. Should anything have gone wrong down in the Everglades, and they traced the vans to him, he could always say they were being used by people in the employ of the nursery. He could even say they were homeless people who he was helping out. That done, they talked about where each of them would go.

The first thing they settled on was to allow Hobbit to be a central news outlet for the six. They would write or call him and tell him the news. He could then distribute it via mail or telephone. This seemed like a grand plan, because each of them thought of the group as a family.

Mary told Hobbit the next morning that she wanted to buy a Jeep. She was still determined to go to Aspen, Colorado, to open a beauty shop, and she would need a four-wheel drive vehicle for the Rocky Mountains. He asked her to drive one of the vans to the paint shop, then they would take a taxi to the Jeep dealership. He was determined to change the color of the vans right away. Later, he would put them in storage for a while. If nothing happened concerning them, he would use them with the nurseries or donate them to the Mission.

Mary got a bright red Jeep. Hobbit joked that she and Jack Frost would make a pair. She told him to kiss her foot, and was about half-serious.

When Mary drove her new Jeep off the lot, she headed straight for the shotgun house. The ones leaving—all of them except Hobbit—had decided that since they had a ten-day grace period they wouldn't register their cars in Florida.

California Red, Little Debbie and Screaming Girl had purchased cars that day, also, and they all showed up at the shotgun house to sport them to Hobbit and Mary the woman. As the evening wore on, the subject turned to where they would hold their going-away party, and Hobbit told them of a house on Treasure Island that he had been looking at. It was on the beach, had four bedrooms and two baths upstairs, a living room, dining room, kitchen and a half-bath down stairs, plus a courtyard surrounded by a ten-foot wall. The courtyard was beautifully planted with Florida fauna. The price was great, too. The owners wanted only three hundred thousand dollars for it.

All being in a good mood, they told him that they would help him furnish it, and they could have their party there. This was pleasing to Hobbit. He agreed to everything, even offered them a room and bed any time in the future that they should be in Florida.

Early the next morning, Hobbit called the real estate person who was selling the house for the owner. He told her that he had looked it over and would buy it. He also told her he wanted to pay in cash and would have the money with him. The transaction would take place in the real estate office. When he arrived at the office that afternoon, she ushered him into a private office, counted the three hundred thousand dollars he offered to her and handed him the papers to the building and property. Everything done. Nothing to it.

That evening, the six went shopping for house furnishings, and paid extra for an early delivery date. Everything would be at the house the next afternoon.

The party they had the following evening rocked the entire island. They invited everyone in who wanted to come in, and sent for more refreshments, dips and potato chips when they were needed. A guest brought in some grass and all users got stoned. The next morning, the usual after-party mess was adorned with persons lying all over the floor, on the couches; most of the people had staggered out before the six began waking, and they went around getting the others up and out. Hobbit swore off party guests. Mary swore off parties. The other four swore.

Hobbit had a cleaning service come in and fix the place up, so that when the other five arrived the next afternoon to hug and say goodbye, the place showed no signs of damage.

Jack Frost was going to Abilene, Texas to open a pawnshop. Mary the woman was still determined to open a beauty parlor in Aspen, Colorado. Screaming Girl said she wanted to go to Price, Utah; Red and Debbie were headed to Watsonville, California to get married and open a restaurant. Hobbit would remain in Florida and open another day care center or two.

Epilogue

Red was having trouble with the bow tie. It just wouldn't work for him. No matter what he tried, the tie wouldn't stay tied.

Knocking on the door, Red's brother asked him if everything was alright.

"Heck no!" he replied. "I can't get this stupid string bow tie to stay tied."

"Want me to help?" his brother asked him.

"Yes!" Red exclaimed in reply.

It took his brother only a minute to fix the tie; then Red put his jacket on.

"First tux I've ever worn," Red said to no one in particular.

"It's what Mom would have wanted," his brother told him. "She would be real proud to see you all dressed up and going to church to get married, especially about the church. Mom never lost her faith that you would come back some day and go back to the church."

"Maybe she's watching," Red told him. "Just maybe she is. God might let her, if it was all that important."

"You've changed a lot, brother. Even during the past year you have changed a lot, and I am glad for it. To hear you speak as a brother in Christ fills my heart with joy."

Red smiled. He knew his brother loved him, always had known it; and now he, too, was glad he knew the Lord.

Debbie was already at the church when Red and his brother got there. Since Red's brother was going to be the best man, he turned toward the front of the church where he and Debbie would walk down the isle. Tracy, his brother's wife, would be the maid of honor. Becky, their daughter, had been invited, but couldn't make it.

When the organist began playing, Red stepped up in front of the Rev. Jim Wright, Pastor of the Missionary Baptist Church, the church Red's brother and sister-in-law were members of. Reverend Wright smiled, and, as the music turned to the beginning strands of "Here Comes the Bride," his eyes lighted up in the direction from which the bride and best man were coming.

Debbie was obviously nervous, but Reverend Wright had told her that all she would have to do would be to answer "I do" to all of the questions. She did, and in a few minutes Mr. and Mrs. Culpepper were embraced in the public kiss that told the world that they belonged to each other and were no longer fair game.

The newlyweds had decided to spend their honeymoon at sea, so they took a cruise ship out of Santa Cruz for Acapulco, Mexico. Debbie had gone off the pill several days before, and she had high hopes that Red would prove to be as fertile as he looked. He did, and a month later Debbie announced that she was pregnant. When little Hobbie was five weeks old, his proud parents took him before the congregation to be christened. Before everyone, Reverend Wright asked Red and Debbie if they were committing the child to God. Both answered yes.

When Hobbit read the letter Debbie had written to him, he wasn't surprised at all. He had been going to church on a pretty regular basis himself, and had witnessed other babies being christened; but it did surprise him to learn that they had named the boy after him. Hobbie was a good name for a kid. Other kids would like that, and girls would like it later on.

Hobbit had a real love for kids, and had opened a free house for working mothers who were seriously strapped for money. He had promoted Sadie to overseer of all the Miracle Hill Nursery Homes, and Willie Mae was her assistant. They also had homes of their own, a blessing both continued to thank the Lord for.

Because of his financial faithfulness to the church and local civic causes, Hobbit had won a position of respect and admiration among the people of Leesburg. He and his dog, Gertie, were the most popular couple in town. Unless the matter would last over an hour, where Hobbit went Gertie went, too.

Mary the woman had become quite successful with her beauty parlor. She, too, had returned to her religious roots and, with the profits she made from her business, she helped to finance a Catholic mission for homeless, displaced and abandoned children.

Screaming Girl had returned to Helper, Utah, where she married the Director of the Gospel Mission there. However, after ten years of marriage, her husband became seriously ill and died a short time later.

When she called Hobbit, he immediately volunteered to call the others, but she said "no," she would call them. She did, however, ask him to hurry on out so he could help with things. He told her he would be on the first flight to Salt Lake City in the morning.

Getting a pet flight for Gertie proved to be a piece of cake. The Tampa airport handled it like the old hands they were, and Gertie, along with Hobbit, went out on the first morning flight to Salt Lake City.

Screaming Girl and a driver from the Mission met Hobbit at the SLC airport. Gertie shook with excitement when she saw Screaming Girl, and Screaming Girl almost cried when she saw the faithful little fat dog.

The hundred and twenty-five mile drive from Salt Lake City to Helper was filled with recounting old memories. No mention was made, however, of the Cajun. That was a memory long since put on ice.

California Red and Little Debbie flew in with their children, then took a rental station wagon to the Mission. The couple had three children, two boys and a girl. Hobbie, the eldest, was almost ten years old. His brother, Skyler, was eight, and their sister, Deborah, was six. Red and Debbie had decided to stop at three.

Jack Frost flew into Denver where Mary the woman picked him up and drove on to Helper, Utah.

As each of them arrived at the Mission, Screaming Girl showed them to their rooms, which she had reserved especially for them. At supper that night, they all had a laugh when someone pointed out that six millionaires were staying in a Rescue Mission for homeless people.

Screaming Girl had not told her husband about the money she had, although she shared each year with the interest she drew on it. Now, actually, she had more than she had when she came to Helper. Her husband had seen to it that her every need was taken care of.

All of the women cried during the graveside services, and the makings of a tear appeared in the eyes of the men. When it was over, the six retired to the Mission.

They had all gone down to the dining room when their conversation turned to religion, and it was during that time that the others offered to stay a while with Screaming Girl until she could get things straightened out. But she declined, saying that she was going to give up Mission work. When asked what she planned to do, she answered, "I don't know."

Immediately, Jack Frost spoke up, saying, "You can come in with me, if you want to."

"How do you mean that?" asked Screaming Girl.

"Well, I'm a Christian now, myself. As a matter of fact, I'm an ordained deacon. So there wouldn't be any fornicating."

Screaming Girl smiled. She knew from the letters they had written over the years that all of them were Christians now. They had even told her about the experiences that had led them to give over to the Lord.

"I'd even marry you," added Jack Frost.

"Let me think on that until tomorrow," Screaming Girl told him.

When the morrow came, Screaming Girl said "Yes," and Jack Frost demanded that all of the others come to their wedding. All accepted the demanded invitation.

Jack Frost decided to stay in Helper for a few days in order to help Screaming Girl get her things together for shipping to Texas; then he would catch the Amtrak home.

Mary the woman invited Hobbit to ride back to Aspen with her, promising to drive him over to Denver when he got ready to leave.

Red and Debbie's children were already excited over the trip to Texas.

Screaming Girl could not just leave Helper without seeing the many friends she had made in Carbon County, Utah. There were meetings to attend, farewell speeches to be made, hugs and kisses for those who had been very close to her.

Jack Frost remained in the background until he caught the Amtrak home. He felt that it would be easier for Screaming Girl if he was not there.

At the end, however, Screaming Girl arrived in Fort Worth, Texas, with a smile on her face and love in her heart for the man who had spoken up for her so many years before. It was a legacy of love that would last far into the next century, a lasting thing.

Hobbit and Mary the woman, along with Gertie, left Helper in Mary's Jeep Cherokee, heading to Aspen, Colorado. By the time they reached Grand Junction, Colorado, conversation had slowed, and even Gertie had taken a break from running from one side of the rear seat to the other in order to look out of the windows.

"What would you say if I asked you to marry me?" Hobbit asked right out of the clear blue.

"I quit cussing," Mary replied.

"No, I'm serious," Hobbit pursued the matter.

"Well, Hobbit," began Mary, "I'm Catholic, and I own a business in Aspen, Colorado. A far piece from Leesburg, Florida."

"But you could sell the business, and live off the interest the cash you have in the bank will bring in," Hobbit interrupted. Then he added, "How much cash do you have?"

"Over a million, probably. I've done real well with the business," Mary replied.

"So have I," Hobbit told her. "I have almost six million in cash."

Then, for a minute neither of them said anything. But finally Mary the woman spoke up. "How much does it matter that I am Catholic?"

"None," he told her, then continued, "I follow the simple wording of the Bible, and the simple wording says that anyone who loves God and his fellow man, and recognizes the supremacy of Christ over the destiny of the human soul, then lives according to the morals, values and ethics of the New Testament is going to spend the remainder of eternity with God.

"I don't believe any one church or denomination has got it all. And I believe that when most people start believing that one does, then that will be when the anti-Christ will come in and take over."

"You always did have a knack for giving simple answers to complicated questions," Mary told him.

"We're just like Jack Frost and Screaming Girl, and California Red and Little Debbie: we cared for each other when we were out after the big score, and we can renew that if we want to."

"Maybe you're right," she told him, "But I'll have to think it over for a while."

"Can I go ahead and buy you a ring?" he asked in a lighthearted way.

"Sure," she told him. "I can always pawn it if I go broke."

Hobbit toyed with the idea of taking a local plane flight from Aspen to Denver, but the thought that he and Gertie might be placed on separate flights at Denver to Tampa caused him to stick with the original plan. Mary the woman would drive him and Gertie to the Denver airport.

When Jack Frost and Screaming Girl finally got things straightened out in Texas, they sent out the invitations for the wedding. It was to be a gala affair with all of the invited guests also invited to a sumptuous dinner at Jack Frost's sprawling ranch-style home.

Hobbit decided not to bring Gertie, because he wanted to spend more time with Mary. It would also afford him the opportunity to give her the engagement ring and formally ask her to marry him.

The wedding was a big success. Everyone had a really swell time, although no alcoholic beverages were served: a stipulation Screaming Girl had made.

Hobbit did give Mary the ring and formally asked her to marry him; but they decided to keep things under wraps in order not to take the edge off Jack Frost and Screaming Girl's marriage.

The newlyweds had decided on Paris for their honeymoon. This would be the first time Screaming Girl had ever been out of the United States.

Again, however, Hobbit went home with Mary and the two spent some time together before Hobbit returned to Florida.

Seven months later Hobbit and Mary the woman announced their forth-coming marriage. The ceremony would take place in the First Baptist Church in Leesburg, Florida, and the couple planned a two-week stay in the Holy Land for their honeymoon.

When the others arrived in Leesburg, Screaming girl almost stole the show with her pregnancy of her first child. Everyone, including Hobbit and Mary the woman, were elated that another new life would be added to the family.

Instead of selling her business, Mary the woman leased it to a young Christian woman, who, like herself, was a cosmetology graduate with a couple of years of experience. The upstairs apartment went with the business, but Mary won a concession for one of the bedrooms to be kept for her in case she wanted to come up for skiing.

After they had packed and shipped all of Mary's things to her new Treasure Island address, the couple decided to drive Mary's Jeep Cherokee back to Leesburg.

There had been snow on the ground when they arrived in Aspen, and Gertie had the time of her life. She had never been out in snow before and the other dogs thought she was crazy, except one in particular. He was a border collie and it was love at first sight. When Hobbit and Mary discovered what had happened, they searched for the owner of the border collie. Finding him, they offered him a lot of money for the dog and he sold it to them.

When they got home to Treasure Island, Gertie taught the border collie how to chase the waves back into the ocean, and pretty soon both of them were finding paper money on the beach and putting it in a large bowl on the back porch of the house.

Although they started trying right away, it was over two years later before Hobbit and Mary had their first child. It was a girl, and they named her Gertie.

About the Author

Thirty years ago George Ellis Wheeler, Jr. rode the rails throughout the western United States. After going to college, he joined a Rescue Mission as a Foodservice Manager. He is a twenty-year member of the Association of Gospel Rescue Missions, formerly the International Union of Gospel Rescue Missions.